CANDY CRONE

THE HAWTHORNE UNIVERSITY WITCH SERIES

A.L. HAWKE

PHANTOM HEART, LLC

ISBN: 978-1-953919-76-2

ISBN: 978-1-953919-73-1 (ebook)

Library of Congress Control Number: 2024919397

This is a work of fiction. It comes directly from the author's imagination. Witchcraft is included to infuse a sense of realism to the novel, but in no way is it supposed to represent actual practicing witchcraft, witches or the religion of Wicca. The book also includes fictitious names, characters, places, and incidents. Any public names are used solely for creative purposes. Any resemblance to actual people, living or dead, or to companies, institutions, or locales is entirely coincidental or accidental.

Line edited by Stephanie Marshall Ward

Proofread by Alexa B., alexabooks.wixsite.com/authors

Cover Design © 2024 by Brosedesignz

Published by Phantom Heart, LLC

27702 Crown Valley Pkwy D-4, #201

Ladera Ranch, CA 92694, USA

Printed and bound in the United States of America

First printing 2024

Learn more about A.L. Hawke at www.alhawke.com

Correspondence: contact@alhawke.com

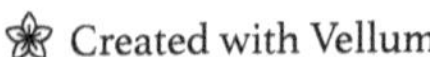 Created with Vellum

1

———

TOTALLY NOT SANTA

I CAN'T DECIDE WHICH IS BETTER. A PEPPERMINT STICK IN A steamy mug of cocoa, with tiny chocolate chips and thick chocolate syrup coating whipped cream, *OR* a cinnamon quill dipped in spicy bright red sauce and swirled caramel over vanilla ice cream in a large frosted silver bowl. I mean, they're both absolute bliss, right? The kick from the caramel apple surprise tastes good—*yum*—but that hot cocoa with the frosty whip is damn good too. So... I mean... I just don't know. My sweetest friend Frida introduced me to this caramel confectionery masterpiece last year, and I've been enjoying it ever since. Honestly, I think they're both to die for.

Whiffs of steam from the hot cocoa warm my face beside this large icy window looking out at all the trees in the surrounding wilderness. No one's walking along the one-way street through the frigid wind and icy snow tonight. Fluffy white blankets of snow coat the sides of the road, and ice flurries are blizzarding. The fresh snow reminds me of my vanilla ice cream. *Ummmm. Yummy.* It is sublime. Yep, I'm at Hawthorne Sweets again. But when I proposed meeting with this prospective student, I had no idea the weather would be so frigidly "anti-ice-cream."

I clutch my red jacket tighter over two layers of sweaters and jeans. *Brr*, it's cold. The weather is so unpredictable in Hawthorne, Georgia, you know. It didn't snow much at all last year.

"Cadence, Dad's fine with the idea now," Cat says across from me in the peach vinyl booth. "I'm telling you, he's fine with me going to college here in Hawthorne."

Do you remember Cat? She's that really fun teenager with pigtails on one side of her head and the other side bald that I met when going on a haunted haunt last year. Well, right now she's growing her hair out. Because she's applying to schools and has an important interview tomorrow. She'd almost look normal, if it weren't for the Gothic makeup. (Who am I to talk? I've got plenty of witchy makeup over my eyes and lips.) And...wait a second, just let me try another dip of this hot red sauce—I mean, shit, it's incredible.

Hawthorne Sweets is so surreal. All the walls on one side of this ice cream parlor are windowed. The other side is painted bright peach, pink, and white. And having this place a block away from my school, in the middle of the forest, is unreal. Not to mention that this season there are a bunch of large peppermint sticks and reindeer decals stuck on the walls. Two waitresses wearing cute peach-colored aprons and red-and-white elf hats are scooping ice cream behind a counter lined with classic silver stools. The place has a distinctive two-columned ice cream cone entrance. But tonight, the ice cream cone statues are covered in balsam fir and a shiny silver wreath with red and green lights. The silver tabletops are decorated for the season with reindeer placemats—mine has a glowing red nose. Until I learned about all our witchy occult secrets, it was a mystery to me why Hawthorne didn't celebrate Christmas. Well, not here at Hawthorne Sweets. Hawthorne Sweets is totally Santa.

"You're right, Cadence," Cat says, spooning luscious chocolate syrupy goo. "This ice cream here is really good."

"Sure is, Cat. Sure is." I swirl some red sauce and vanilla.

"After what happened at the Billington House," Cat says with a mouth full, "dad wants me to come to school here too."

"You gotta think of your studies," I say, shaking my head and laughing. "Your future's what's important, Cat, not magic stuff in Hawthorne. And they might not even accept you here."

"My grades are good enough. The interview isn't about getting in, it's all about the scholarship. I'm already in Hawthorne."

"You're meeting with Dr. Kahn?" I sip my hot cocoa. Then I rub my protruding belly thinking of my unborn baby, Chandra. This stuff is great and all, but I might be looking at quite a bellyache for me and you, darling. "Dr. Kahn's a good history professor, one of my favorites. Just talk to him about the Shang dynasty." I swirl my spoon in the red sauce and lick it. "He's fascinated by China. Talk about Confucius. Maybe . . ." I wag my silver spoon at her in thought. "Throw in some Confucian philosophy stuff."

"See, Cadence, you're already helping."

"Well, if you're accepted, you can't join my coven. I already have twelve sisters."

"Cadence!" She grunts and hits the table. "Why not?"

"The circle's complete," I say with a shrug. "Forget witchcraft and just focus on your studies."

"Sweets for little children to eats?"

What the hell? The words are jarring coming from a

pale, wrinkled lady shuffling down the row of booths, repeating the words over and over again.

"Sweets for children to eat? Sweets for children to eats?"

She's wearing a raggedy earthy-brown sweater over a gray dress and a black cloth headdress. There's a mark on her long nose. Like a wart. I've seen this lady rummaging through the trash cans on campus. I didn't think much of it then, but right now, crouched over and squinting at us, she looks like your classic image of a witch.

She's going by each booth handing people small candy canes in plastic wraps.

"Growly, growler," she keeps muttering while handing out treats to kids. "Growly, growler."

She stops by a booth behind Cat with two kids and their mom.

"Sweets for children to eats?" she asks again with a chuckle. "Hmm? Make 'em plump. Make 'em strong. So they may run, run, run along."

The boy and girl lurch back. Then the old lady raises a finger, digs in a pocket in her dress, and thrusts more small candy canes toward them.

"Would you care for one, my little one?" she asks the boy. Then she turns to the little girl. "And my, my, what's your name, child?"

"Miley," squeaks the kid.

"Miley? Such a name. Stout. Strong. Have you been good? Have you been behaving?" The hag leans a bit too close to Miley's face. "Being nice for... *Santy Claus*?" Then she explodes into laughter. The little girl nods her head nervously while her mom glares at the crone. "'Tis the Yule season of joy. There'll be no Krampus for you. Krampus runs with his birch rods punishing naughty children, he does. But there will be no Krampus for you."

The little girl shyly nods her head again.

"Would you like to try one?"

The girl nods and reaches over, but her mom snatches her hand.

"No, thank you," says the mother. Then she shakes her head at her daughter. "Miley, no. You have your ice cream."

"Growly, growler," says the old woman, tossing another two small plastic bags on their table. "Growly, growler."

She shrugs and walks on.

Oh no. Our booth's next.

"How about you?" the woman asks us. "But...oh my!" She opens her eyes wide and points at my belly. "Appears you've been eating a bit too many sweets already, child."

"I'm pregnant," I say.

"Pregnant?" she says with a grimace. Then she opens her eyes wide. "Pregnant? And at such a wondrous time." She extends her arms, looking up at the ceiling. "Some parts, ole St. Nicholas has his competition on this night, he does. Others far in the North, by the North Pole, see so many people rushing through the streets laughing and swatting all the kids' asses. They parade in groups under smoke and fire wearing the heads of goats. Rushing down the streets in horns and fur baring sharp teeth. But not here. No, no, not here. No birch rod where all the children are nice and so well behaved. No birch rod whipping for you."

She offers me and Cat two small candy canes in plastic wrappers. We take them just to be polite. I'm a bit repulsed glancing at the old lady's fingers with all that dirt and muck on her skin.

Cat reaches into her small purse and hands a few dollars to the old woman. The woman becomes too cheery, opening her eyes wide.

"Oh, my, oh my! Bless you! Bless you, child. No birch rod for you!"

Then the hag roars with laughter again. And she reaches into her dress and hands Cat a large chocolate cookie. It actually looks like a fresh chocolate chip brownie cookie, but I'm guessing Cat isn't about to take a bite, as bewildered as I am as to where the old lady got it from.

"Excuse me, miss," says one of the waitresses behind her.

"Yes, dearie?" the old hag cocks her head back.

"You can't offer people food in our restaurant."

"Why? On such an upstanding evening?" She puts her finger to her lips. "Tonight he comes. He comes, shh...the goat comes bringing cookies and cakes and candy to all the lucky boys and girls. And they enjoy it so. Just to bring a smile to the little ones' lips. But . . . don't be naughty." She turns and looks deeply into my eyes. A dark shadow is cast over her. It feels cold. "Woe to those who are naughty. He swats them. He takes his birch sticks out and hits 'em. And what do you think we do out here to kids misbehaving in the woods? Grýla stirs her pot. Boil boggled and broggled. Fresh and plump. I keep the pot nice and warm for all those naughty, naughty little children."

"Sweets for children to eats!" she calls out again, continuing farther down the aisle. "Sweets for children to eats." And then more quietly, under her breath, she keeps repeating, "growly growler. Growly growler."

She tosses more candy canes on a couple's table by the exit and then, thankfully, exits out the door.

"She was weird," Cat says.

She sure was. That's how weird it gets in Hawthorne, I suppose. I've seen even stranger. But, as usual, Cat's the kind of person who hardly minds; she's grinning, seemingly loving it. That's Cat. She and her father have been ghost hunting all her life. She lives for weird stuff like this.

But she moves the old crone's chocolate cookie very far from her dish, near the napkin dispenser.

"Tell me more about Doctor Kahn, Cadence. I told you, I'm here no matter what, and you can't convince me otherwise. Even if you don't let me into your coven. But I need more gems for my interview tomorrow."

I dip my spoon in my ice cream. Then I take a swig of hot chocolate.

"Hmm?" I ask, chewing on a chocolate chip. "I only had one class with him, but Maddie had a few. You should ask Maddie. I think . . . he also lectures a lot about the Han dynasty. Chinese history is his specialty. Look a little into ancient China tonight. I heard he likes to emphasize the impact of this dynasty in the development of China's organization and government. So, I'd—"

There's a high-pitched scream. It's from the booth closest to the exit. Then I hear cackling from that weird woman again, this time right outside the window. The hag rushes by our window, clutching her headdress tightly over her head, as ice and wind blow hard against her face.

Cat jumps. "Eww! Look, Cadence!" She points at the small plastic wrappers that woman gave us, only there aren't any candy canes. The candy canes have been transformed into squiggly brown worms, rubbing against the clear plastic wrappers.

"Oh, gross! Look!" Cat points at the cookie.

The cookie that crone handed Cat is now just a small mound of mud with white maggots wiggling around and a couple flies swarming it.

There's crying. It's coming from the booth behind Cat. It's the little girl.

"Mommy, my stomach hurts."

2

—————

HAPPY HALLOWEEN

"Be gentle, Cadence," my best friend Maddie warns. We make our way up a paved walkway. There's a brick facade on the front of the single-story home. Maddie and I are wearing thick, heavy coats, and the path leading to the front door is lined by fluffy white snow, covering the bushes and grass. It's not as stormy anymore, but it's really cold. "If she carries on, just let her keep talking. Don't challenge what she says. And don't jump in talking about the candy canes. You haven't seen her since Mom's wedding, and she's still real confused." Then she lifts a hand, ready to knock, but first turns to me. "Be slow and be patient. And . . . whatever you do, don't talk about witches, okay?"

"How am I going to mention the other night if I can't talk about witches, Maddie?"

"Well, I told you that you shouldn't come if you're just here to get information from her. She might be confused, but she's sharp, as bright as you. Maybe hint, but don't be direct. She can't take talking about witchcraft. If you get her too angry, well, she won't fight you with magic, but she'll clam up. She didn't say a word or eat for three days after Mom last mentioned Geneva Forest. So . . . are you ready?"

"Not after your telling me all this."

"You'll be fine," Maddie says with a chuckle, touching my arm. "She loves it when Mom and I come and visit. I think she'll love seeing you. I mean, she wouldn't be here if it weren't for you."

An older woman with long red hair and glasses opens the door. We remove our thick coats and put them on hooks by the door. Then we take off our boots, wet with ice. Inside, the place is warm. It smells like chicken soup. It's dark even though most of the drapes are open. I think the darkness is because it's cloudy outside. We pass a lady with a yellow-dyed crew cut and rings on her nose and lips watching TV near the kitchen. A disheveled lady is pacing back and forth by a saffron-curtained window, wearing a T-shirt and sweat-pants. Then we pass a room with a woman in gray sweat-pants and a T-shirt on the carpet brushing paint on a canvas. I peek at the painting. It's a lady in a long black dress and tall black hat sitting beside a cat. The artwork is a bit strange, but really good. Finally, in the room at the end of the hall, a figure with long golden-blond hair in light blue pajamas is sitting in a fluffy brown corduroy lounge chair. There's an open bag of chips lying on the floor, a few stray tortilla chips, and a bunch of lit candles on a table with a tray of uneaten food. She's just staring through the window.

"Hi, Melanie," Maddie says.

"Hi, Madison," Melanie mutters. She still stares, but her lips curl into a smile. "Hi, Cadence. So nice for you to visit me. Happy Halloween."

"Merry Christmas, Melanie," Maddie corrects. "How are you doing?" She reaches down and hugs her. "Mom found some work for you near Pooler. We thought getting you a job might help you feel a little better. Or did you start work at the local laundromat? That's just down the street, right?"

"Aha," Melanie says. "See. I already started quilting." She points to the blanket over her body. "I love sewing. First thing I ever sewed was Winnie's stomach. When her doll was all flayed open, I tied the skin real taut. Remember, Momma?"

She finally breaks her stare and looks at me.

"Sure, Melanie. Sure."

"You're not my momma," Melanie snarls, shaking her head.

But then she weirdly reaches out for me to hug her.

"It's nice to see you again," Melanie says in my embrace. "How are you, Cadence?"

"I'm fine, Melanie. Fine. You're doing okay?"

"Things are nice. Very nice. But things aren't going so well back home in Hawthorne I hear?"

"No, everything is fine."

Melanie shakes her head.

"Cadence just wanted to visit with me this time," Maddie says.

"You, Madison, maybe, but not her. Why would Kathy come all the way through the cold snow to see me? Bonnie tells me she ain't never remembered the roads being this icy. Lammas was colder than ever. What's happening with the weather lately? I think God's planning some sort of punishment. I think the heat changing to cold means something's going on with God. God's probably fighting Satan again. God's always fighting Satan. It probably means the first break of the seals. Of course, it's warm inside, isn't it? Thanks to God."

She smiles and buries her head in her hands. Then she

starts shaking. *Is she laughing?* Maddie glances at me, flashing a rueful grin.

Melanie, once called the Samhain Witch, was the most powerful witch in the world. The witch council couldn't control her. Neither could my mentor witch, Alondra. It was only when I developed the talent of seeing demons—something I'd rather not have seen—that I helped her. That's when she nearly choked me to death.

Did I help her? According to Madison and Aunt Jane, she spends all her time just sitting by this window. Maybe she would have been better off living like Bigfoot, as her muddy, smelly self under the shelter of mud and leaves in our forest?

"Been cryin' lately?" Melanie asks me. She lifts those black eyes, gazing right into mine, reminding me of her ego witch-self. I quickly shake my head. "People never stop their crying. They cry and cry and cry. But they never really stop crying. Even after babies grow, the tears never stop falling. They still cry." Thankfully, she breaks her gaze. "When I was little, Winona used to cry a lot. Mommy sure would get upset at all of her crying. You know what I'd say? I'd say—wagging my finger—'now, Winnie, you do what Momma tells you or else. No use cryin' all the time.' And she knew what I meant, she sure did. She never crossed me after I learned how to play with black stars and crosses. You can always take sticks from those sigils and stop everybody from crying."

Maddie nods, standing over her, forcing an uncomfortable grin.

"Back when all the other kids went playing with fire trucks, riding bikes or playing with boards, Winnie and I would go out with our special deck of cards. I'd rummage through the cards giving everyone a reading. Got to the time when I was pretty darn good at playing cards. Got to be that it always came true. Everything. I'm really good at playing cards, Cadence. That's why I know you're not just visiting to see me. You understand, sometimes a flush is a flush, a full house is a full house, and it just ain't worth nothin' bettin' too much money when you're destined to lose. Just like it ain't worth nothin' to try to stop folks from crying. They still cry. But Winona and Daddy always lost when betting cards against me. Because I was pretty good, and I didn't cry so much back then. Remember, Momma?"

She weirdly looks up at me again as if I'm her mom.

She's so weird. Her body looks so delicate and thin in her blue pajamas and with that blanket over her body—but not her eyes. Those eyes are terrifying. The obsidian orbs gaze right into you. Intelligent, just like Maddie said, but menacing. She might be rambling like a lunatic, but I feel like there's a part of her that's ready to lash out and tear my throat out again. But, even creepier, she also seems ready to burst into laughter.

Is she talking nonsense? Genius? I'm not sure. All I know is she scares the hell out of me.

Her eyes turn vacant. But because she keeps looking at me, I hesitantly shake my head again.

"It was hard for Mom and Dad and my sister when I was little," she says with a nod, looking back to the window. "It's hard to stop the crying. The crying really never ends until you're under dirt, and then, well . . . you just can't hear them tears fall anymore."

She grips her head in her hands, and her whole body shakes again.

"Melanie," I say hesitantly. "I came because I wanted to ask you about Christmas. There's a Christmas witch that did a curse at an ice cream parlor, seeming to hurt a little girl.

Do you know of an old witch that attacks children during the Christmas season? When you haunted Halloween, did another witch haunt Christmas afterward? This witch referred to herself as *Grýla*, like the Icelandic witch. I asked Kenosha, but she was unsure."

Melanie freezes with her head still in her hands. Then she quickly shakes—not just her head, her whole body.

"No, Kates," Maddie mutters quietly, shaking her head. "No, not now."

"A Yule witch, or—"

"Help yourselves to eating," Melanie says, looking up with a big smile. Then she stretches out her arms and yawns. She gestures to a sandwich on a paper plate on the table as if no one said anything. "They always make me bologna sandwiches for lunch. I mean, you can add mustard, but, I mean, come on. Bologna sandwiches? Just plain white bread and bologna and they call that lunch. I told Bonnie time and time again that I fuckin' hate bologna, but there it is. Just as there be bologna in Hawthorne, there be bologna in my goddamn bedroom. See?"

"This witch is turning candy into worms," I add.

Melanie quickly shakes her head. But I stop talking when Melanie buries her head in her hands again.

"No, Cadence," Maddie snaps. "No."

"Melanie," Maddie drawls, taking a knee beside her chair and gently touching her shoulder. "Why don't we go over your money arrangements? Mom and I are going to help you get an account."

Melanie looks up. "But I don't have any money, Madison," she says with tears running down her cheeks. She looks so sad.

"I know," Maddie says, "I know. But you will. You said

you're working at the laundromat. We should discuss financial arrangements."

"I was only joking about all that," she says with a laugh. "I'm not working in the laundromat."

"Well . . . you're going to start work soon," Maddie says. "And when you do, you're going to need to be saving."

"You're so nice."

"Willow suggested . . ." I continue.

"Stop it, Cadence!" Maddie snaps. "Shut up! What did I tell you?"

"A child was hurt by magic, Maddie," I object. "That little girl looked like her stomach was in pain after eating the worm."

"Ever cut open a stomach?" Melanie asks. "Get plenty of worms that way. Worms and blood and a horrible smell. They're all there underneath the skin, muscles, and bones, if you take a look. Not really something anybody bothers to talk about, not even doctors. It's like smashing pumpkins and tearing out all that sinew and pumpkin. But I'd rather not talk about worms and ice cream. Please tell her to stop talking about worms and ice cream, Madison."

"Never mind, Melanie," Maddie says gently. "Never mind." Then Madison looks up at me, seeming ready to slug me. "Mom and I are planning to get you an account. So I think that. . ."

I grip my hand tightly. But then. . . I venture to the window.

It's pleasant watching the snowflakes slowly fall outside. A table on a small concrete patio is now covered in a blanket of snow. Beyond a bunch of old suburban houses is a small park with a bunch of trees with hanging moss. I love Spanish moss on trees. It makes Savannah so pretty. I remember Kenosha talking about the trees in New Orleans that have moss like that. Hawthorne is too far up in elevation to have trees like that.

"Growly, growler," Melanie says.

I whirl around.

"What did you say?" I snap. "That's what that witch said in the ice cream parlor."

"What?" Melanie asks.

"*Growly, growler.* You said *growly, growler.*"

"But she won't be bothering your nice friends," Melanie says. "Your friends are all grown up. That handsome husband of yours, Bryce, and your brother, Damien. Even Madison's mom and your nice dad. All the old people are safe. They cry a lot, but they keep it all inside. That's of no use for Yule. But not a child. Or a newborn baby. They're just ripe enough. And you're beginning to show, aren't you, Cadence? That could be something."

"Is Grýla going to threaten my baby, Melanie?"

When she turns to the window ready to go mum again, it's too much. I rush right over and turn her toward me. She stares at my hands, which are holding her. A flicker of rage erupts on her face. In a flash, I'm reminded of how dangerous she is.

"It's not fair," Melanie drawls, still staring at my hands, "when they want to take something so cute and cuddly, so sweet, and turn it sour."

"What's she going to do to my baby? What, Melanie? What are you talking about? You said '*growly, growler.*' How did you know that phrase?"

"Well . . . Yuletide . . . is a cold time, Windstorm. Over the years, hope was always that crops and wheat would grow so people wouldn't starve to death. That's why we celebrate the light at the end of the maze. Anyone who wishes to get the energies during this part of the year is going to be feeding on children in preparation for Imbolc. They're looking for fire to light the lampshade. Sometimes seven candles will do, other times, just one, the one in the center of your chest. Like you and your baby, Chandra."

"How do you know my baby's name!"

She's freaking me out. I feel panicked. Maddie's looking worried now too.

"I'm just saying, it's not all about stockings and candy and fat, jolly gremlins making their way down chimneys eating cookies and handing out gifts. It's that feeling you get. It's that nice warm baby-fresh feeling. Like smelly diapers and pee. Just like your friend Madison here."

"You've never heard of a Christmas witch this time of year?"

"I *sure* don't want to be talking about witches."

"But how did you know that phrase: *growly, growler*?"

"Madison sure is right," Melanie says, weirdly opening her eyes wide, "I sure don't like talking about witches." She smiles and touches my hand. "You know, Olivia and Tiffany are such friendly roommates. Did you meet them? Tiffany's a really good drawer. She loves drawing. Ask her to draw something for you. She drew me a drawing of me sitting in this chair when it was clear and sunny outside. It was so pretty. And she drew another of a vase and flowers. Isn't that great? Just a vase with flowers. She called it a . . . still life. I don't understand why people like drawing dead flowers, but they sure are pretty. And why is it called still life? Cause it's still? Like dead? Did she show you her art with dead flowers? Ask Tiffany to draw one of her dead flowers for you. And Olivia, well, she makes me laugh—"

"Melanie, is Grýla going to hurt Chandra?"

"Selfish," Melanie snaps, turning back to the window. She folds her arms. "Don't like talking about witches.

Navitas Nativitatis. Navitas Nativitatis. Navitas Nativitatis. Per dominum. Per dominum. What more can I say? It's like tarot. All this talk about witches leads to witchcraft. Then you fight witches with witchcraft, and magic makes witches turn to witches. Which you apparently wish a witch to be? Stop all your crying." She shakes her head. "Be brave. I never really thought there could be good witches in the world, but when you helped me, Cadence, I saw you were a good witch. So are you, Madison. So is your mom. I like you witches. If it wasn't for you, I would still be left out in the cold."

"We like you too, Melanie," Maddie says. "She'll stop talking about all this. *Won't you*, Cadence?"

"But . . . does she want—"

"Which or witches. Spells spell spells."

"Melanie," Maddie says. "We just want you to be well."

"But Melanie—"

Melanie turns to me with a blank stare. She looks confused. While Maddie looks angrier at me than ever. So . . . I lose my nerve.

"It's," I say with a sigh, "it's really good seeing you again, Melanie."

"So nice for you to visit me, Cadence. Happy Halloween."

3

———

WITCH HUNTING

Bryce and I pass between that two-columned entrance with ice cream statues, converted to giant Christmas trees, by the entrance to Hawthorne Sweets. Mira and Kenosha aren't far behind. I glance back at them; they look so intense. That makes me laugh. Hey, what do you get when four witches walk into an ice cream bar ready to open up a can of witch whoop ass? Either a real bad joke or a gunslinging paranormal movie. I know we're worried about this new witch in town, but walking into an ice cream parlor ready for a magic brawl seems silly.

Mira raises her eyebrows at me. But Bryce gets my mirth, smiling. So I take my hubby's hand.

We are passing two peach vinyl booths full of college students blissfully gorging on ice cream. It's late, so the other booths are empty.

"Hi, Doctor Trent," a student says to Kenosha.

"Oh, hello, Owen," says Kenosha with a smile. Kenosha's wearing a wig and looks professorly, instead of like a bald witch, because we're only a block away from campus.

"Hi, Professor Wallace," says another boy in a red Hawthorne sweater.

"Hi, Kai," Bryce says.

I head over to a middle-aged lady wearing a red felt hat with a white pom-pom and a peach dress and apron wiping down a silver stool. She was here when Cat and I ate here last time.

"Excuse me, miss? Do you remember that elderly woman stopping by here offering people candy canes?"

"Yes. I told her she can't hand out food to our customers."

"Has she been back?" asks Kenosha.

"No, thank goodness. She left a trail of trash. Would you all like a booth? You can take any open table you'd like."

"Which table were you sitting at, Cadence?" asks Kenosha.

I point to a now-vacant booth. And we sit in the same place I sat with Cat, only this time Bryce is beside me and Kenosha and Mira are across from us. Then I grab one of the laminated menus leaning by the napkin dispenser. It's usually the same large pictures of those same incredible sundaes but, this month, it's full of hollies and fir leaves and pictures of Santa Claus and his reindeer.

"Where on the table was the transmutation?" asks Kenosha.

"The candy canes were by our ice cream bowls," I say, putting a finger on my chin. "And the cookie . . . I think, well . . . I'm sure Cat's cookie turned into mud right there by the window."

"*Revelare*," Mira says with a nod, closing her eyes and running her fingers near the napkin holder. "*Revelare*. Reveal the Christmas witch."

"Christmas witch, Mira?" I laugh. "I thought the circle agreed on Grýla?"

"Cadence, stop laughing at all this," Mira says. "Afreyea arranged this investigation for the council."

"Sorry," I say with a shrug. "I just think *Christmas Witch* sounds funny."

"Why has your circle decided on calling this witch Grýla, Cadence?" Kenosha asks.

But my cellphone rings in my small purse before I can reply. I dig in the bag and look. It's Raymond, Cat's dad. He's probably checking on how my meeting with his daughter went. But before I can answer, the call drops.

"We have to call her something," Bryce says with a shrug. "Legend has it that Grýla disguised herself as a beggar in order to gather up the naughty children to boil in her pot. It fits Katie's description. That old lady was up to no good with the kids. And the witch even called herself by that name, Kates said. She said she stirs a pot for naughty children."

"And she kept saying '*Growly, growler*,'" I say with a nod. "It was weird coming from a normally quiet homeless woman wandering campus. It's like she was acting more like a witch than even the Samhain Witch. This witch is old and wears tattered clothing. She's even got a wart on her nose. I mean, Melanie was covered in mud, which was terrifying enough, but this lady looks *textbook* witch."

"What about our former Halloween Witch?" asks Kenosha. "Did the Samhain Witch have any idea what all this was about?"

"A whole lot of nothing. Melanie rambled on and on, talking nonsense. She's crazy. But at one point, Melanie said *growly, growler*. That got my attention. When I pressed her on it, she said all my sisters were safe, but she hinted that the witch might go after my unborn baby. I kept asking her about that—'cause that totally freaked me out—but she wouldn't explain much further. Or at least she didn't say anything else that made much sense. The only thing I could make out was Melanie talking about energies during this Christmas season, dark energies, that grow by feeding on children."

"Grýla is just an Icelandic myth, Windstorm," Mira says. "It's folklore."

"But it sounds like our witch knows the folklore too," objects Kenosha, nodding pensively. Then Kenosha weirdly closes her eyes and runs her fingers over the table. She breathes in and out, focusing deeply, like Mira did before.

"Did you all decide on something?" asks the waitress.

"I'll have your caramel apple surprise," I say. "Maybe with some extra red hot syrup. It's so good."

"Two spoons," Bryce says to the waitress, lifting two fingers.

The waitress looks at Mira and Kenosha. After Kenosha bobs her head up and down a few times with her eyes closed, the waitress gets the hint and leaves.

"I don't feel anything," Kenosha says finally, heaving a sigh.

"Well, the ice cream here is amazing," I say, putting my menu back behind the dispenser. "You should really try some, Kenosha. Chandra loves it. When I taste sugar, she goes crazy in my belly."

"Did you see any demons around the witch?" Kenosha asks me.

"Samhain or Grýla?"

"Either."

"I always see demons." But then I remember seeing a shadow cover Grýla. "Yes . . . when the witch met my gaze standing over this booth, a shadow was cast over her. Yeah, demons were behind her. She felt very evil."

"How about now?"

I really don't want to. Necromancy is a talent I never wanted. The only other witch I know that can see demons like I can is Melanie, and look what the talent did to her.

See that black shade lying flat against the wall as if he's just a leftover Halloween prop? You might mistake him for a torn old costume if it weren't for his bright white eyes. There's another bunched up on the ceiling by the door. They never move. The only things that stir are their shredded, tattered bodies as they flutter like flags in the wind.

"They're here," I say. "So, Kenosha?"

"Are there more in this restaurant than usual?" asks Kenosha.

"No."

"You said that you had a dream after the transmutation?" asks Kenosha. "Like a witch wandering, Cadence?"

"In my dream," I reply thoughtfully with a nod, "I thought I was in another witch wandering. I was walking in the dark forest around my house. Snow was on the ground, but I felt warm, even though I had disrobed. I . . . I felt threatened. Usually in my wanderings, I feel empowered. Not in this dream. That's what made me feel like I was being hunted. When I started feeling too creeped out, I stopped and hunted for large sticks and branches. I piled them one on top of another and formed the shape of a pentagram, then glided a stick in the mud creating a circle around it. That was weird. I have no idea why I did that. And, weirder, all the while, I kept hearing babies crying."

"It sounds like you were casting a shield spell," Kenosha suggests.

"You might have been protecting against oneiromancy,"

Mira says. "This witch might have been attacking you in your dreams, Cadence, like Enora and Melanie once did."

"But the strangest thing is Cadence and I have seen this homeless woman rummaging through trash cans on campus," Bryce says. "Katie's description perfectly matches the lady. If it's the same woman, that old lady is harmless. She minds her own business."

"That's why I asked about demons, Bryce," suggests Kenosha. "It could be a demon possession."

"You thought Cadence was possessed," he objects.

"In a way, she was," Kenosha says. "By achieving mastery over her demons, Cadence was able to rid herself of Alondra's spirit. Melanie was possessed too. We all saw the Samhain Witch's transformation after Cadence defeated her. Part of her 'muddiness' left her."

The waitress comes over with my huge sundae. Wow, three huge scoops of vanilla ice cream are buried under all this hot red syrup, caramel, and chocolate chips. And the cinnamon stick is totally like the cherry on top. I think I could eat this every night. I don't have to worry so much about overeating being pregnant. Right?

But first, I pass the large frosty silver bowl to the love of my life. I watch Bryce take a spoonful of that spicy apple sauce over the vanilla ice cream. Then I do the same with the cinnamon stick, instead of a silver spoon. And it's . . . incredible. Wow. It's that perfect mix of spiciness, tart apple, and vanilla.

"The only magic I witnessed was the transformation of candy into worms," I say with my mouth full of ice cream. "That doesn't strike me as someone powerful like Melanie. But I contacted you guys after Cat and I saw the little girl's mom have to help her into the car that night. We were worried about the girl. You guys sure you don't want some ice cream? There's plenty. Frida got me to love this dish."

"Did you get a hint of the location in the forest in your dream?" Kenosha asks.

"No."

We turn pensive. Except Bryce. He's clanging his silver spoon against the silver dish, eating more of my amazing dessert.

"When I spoke with Afreyea, guys," Mira says, "the headmaster of the witch council was very worried. Something about the transmutation of candy bothered her. Even if all that witch is doing is terrifying little children and causing stomachaches, messing with kids is enough for us to get involved. Afreyea even suggested that she visit us from all the way over in Cotonou to investigate."

"Cadence, you're the Hawthorne Witch," Kenosha says to me. "It's your responsibility to keep this magic under control. We can't wait for Afreyea to travel here from Africa."

"I know," I say. "I don't want a witch in Hawthorne harming kids."

"We have to find her," Kenosha says with a nod, "and meet with her. See what she or her possessor desires. That's what our council's been doing for centuries with rogue witches. That's what I was asked to do with my Crescent coven when investigating Alondra years ago."

"I'll search the woods with you tonight," Mira says.

My phone buzzes, vibrating the purse by my hip. I pull it out again and silence the ringer.

"If it's a demon possession, we need to exorcise it," Kenosha adds. "If she's turned criminal, like Enora, we need to turn her over to the police. If insane, like Melanie, she needs help. Either way, we have to find her and stop this negative presence in Hawthorne."

I glance down at my phone; the contact reads *Raymond* again. A text message reads: *Emergency. Please answer.*

And the phone vibrates again.

"Ray?" I ask, putting my phone up to my ear.

"Cadence, Catrina's missing," Raymond blurts out. "I haven't heard from her since the day she arrived. Of course, Cat has her way of roaming for a day or two, but now I'm really worried. Did she tell you she might be staying somewhere else in Hawthorne?"

"No."

"That's what I was afraid of. I called the hotel and, even though I booked the room, they couldn't tell me much more due to privacy. You know Cat's crazy, but even when she left home and crossed the border into Mexico, she told me exactly where she was. She knows I worry. Her last words were that she was going into Hawthorne Forest to investigate some haunting. She texted it was the biggest supernatural thing she had ever seen. Did she tell you about something going on in Hawthorne Forest?"

"No."

He goes silent.

"My friends and I will do everything we can," I say.

"I'm driving down to Hawthorne now."

"You can stay at our house, Raymond."

I look over at Bryce. He nods.

"That'd be—" He takes a deep breath. "That'd be great, Cadence. Cat looks up to you so much. This time, it's more than a ghost investigation. It's my daughter. Her last message made no sense. It just read *growly, growler*. Do you have any idea what that means?"

I sure do. But before I can tell him, the phone goes dead. Though horrible timing, this isn't so unusual. It's happened many times before on the drive to our desolate college town.

I put my head in my hands and run my fingers through my long hair.

"What is it, Cadence?" Bryce asks, rubbing my back.

"She took Cat."

"Who?" asks Kenosha.

"Grýla."

"How do you know?" asks Mira.

"Cat's last text to her dad read *growly, growler*."

"Told you this was serious, Cadence," Mira says. "This isn't just about candy causing stomachaches."

"We've gotta find her. God, he said she told him she was heading into the forest to investigate. She's probably lost in Hawthorne Forest. If anything happens to Cat, I feel responsible. I only made her more excited about Hawthorne and witchcraft when I met her for that ghost haunting last year. If she's hurt, it'll be all my fault."

"That's nuts," Mira says. "None of this is your fault."

"We have to look for her tonight. Cat is out there in the cold."

"Hawthorne Forest is over a hundred square miles," Kenosha says, shaking her head. "Your friend is literally a needle in a haystack. I suggested Mira and I wander a little to look for this witch too, but I meant locally and with magic, and I thought weeks, even months, not days . . . I'll contact the council. Afreyea should come here."

"But you said it yourself, Kenosha. There's no time."

"Cadence, you can at least wait till morning," Kenosha objects. "Tomorrow morning. Not now. This is the coldest it's been all year and you're pregnant. You might dream walk in the forest at night, but you and your baby won't do well searching for real out there in the cold. Get rest. Mira and I can do more searching tonight around campus."

"I'll go too," Bryce says.

"If she's not near the college, we'll regroup with the entire coven in the morning," Kenosha says with a nod.

I'm staring down at my ice cream. Somehow this amazing red-and-white caramelly delight isn't so wonderful anymore.

"Will you, please, listen to me just this once, Cadence?" Kenosha asks.

I nod slowly.

The trees outside are in shadows in the dark night. It's not snowing, and the moon is shining through clouds, but I think of how bitingly cold it is, seeing all the ice still piled along the street. I will my eyes to see the dark demons. For Cat, I'll do that. Demons thrive in darkness, and right now they're all over the trees outside the window, in hiding. And that means they're all over the wilderness around Cat. One tall, lanky demon is creepily just standing on the street watching me with its creepy bright white eyes.

I jump when Bryce puts his arm around me. He flashes a rueful grin. So I lean my head on his shoulder.

"We have to find her, Bryce. We just have to."

4

———

MIDNIGHT BLUE

I'M SLOWLY WALKING ALONG A NARROW STREET WALLED BY three-story buildings where everything is shaded a midnight blue. Even the streetlights hanging down over me shine indigo. So many windows open into one another from across a teal cobblestone road.

The path winds, and I pass an adjoining street. Here water unnaturally flows very slowly from a large central stone fountain reflecting white-chocolate moonlight. And all is quiet—except for a baby crying.

On the next street, the moon is just bright enough to flash a glance at my own reflection on a shop window. I'm naked, but I feel warm. It's almost as if this dark blue is enough to clothe me. The street widens enough here for small tables and chairs to be laid out. All is still. Except the sound of a baby crying.

White light brightens across another fork in the road, and a large black cat crosses my path. It just stands still amidst the pale turquoise shade. Then the cat shakes, crouches down, and slowly lengthens into a large naked dark-skinned man. But before I can get a better look, the man darts off on all fours.

I pass a shop window revealing a lovely skirt and blouse on a faceless mannequin in front of rows of hangers. On the opposite side of the street is a café. Through the windows I see chairs leaning on empty tables inside dark halls.

I hear footsteps. Someone's following me.

I turn and a tall naked dark-skinned man is standing beside me with sapphire eyes gazing down into mine. Light blue, almost aqua, shines over his ripped chest, large arms, and broad shoulders. His eyes make me feel so calm. There is such warmth in his gaze. I let him run two fingers slowly along my cheek. The fingers wander over my lips, and I run my tongue along his fingers. They taste sweet, as if dipped in maple syrup. Then his fingers, now wet from my lips, run slowly down my neck and along the curve of my breast. Some of his syrup drips on my skin. He bends down and licks my nipple and then sucks my breast. And I embrace him too, desiring him. I want so much to kiss those lips again, to taste the sweetness, desiring that sugar, so I lift his head back and press those soft lips against mine. All the while his fingers probe, massaging deep into my skin, sliding down the slippery curves of my breasts and hips, down to my ass.

Cold stone presses along my back as I'm gently pushed against a hard wall. His eyes shine brighter. And under shining blue light, his torso now shines aqua.

He presses harder into me. His whole body, sticky and wet, as if bathed in molasses, pushes into me. With strong hands, he squeezes the crack of my ass. I reach down and run my fingers over hard muscular abs, while my other hand runs along the muscles over his back. He pinches my butt hard again, almost hurting me. I close my eyes and bring my lips back to his face, ravenously tasting all that sweet stickiness, licking syrupy sweat off his skin. He tastes so sweet. But then . . . my tongue feels fur.

I don't recall facial hair?

Opening my eyes, I can't see his face. His head has disappeared. But I feel something contract against my chest, heavy in my arms.

I'm holding a black cat!

I throw the cat off and he lands on his hind legs. He turns, raises his back, and hisses, then he darts off down an adjacent alley, like that man on all fours did before.

My eyes open to flickering candlelight surrounding my bed in my dark bedroom. I lit these candles when I focused all my intent to cast magic to help my friends. I was scrying to find Cat with dream magic. I asked Hecate to conjure a spell in my sleep to help find her in the forest by scrying. Seems I summoned the wrong cat.

5

ALONDRA'S OFFICE

It's seven-fifty on Wednesday morning. And, well—
yawn—you know, I hate mornings. Of course, it doesn't help
that I didn't sleep at all last night. Between my failed dream
spell and worrying like crazy all night about Bryce and my
friends, there was no sleeping last night. But teaching
assistant Cadence Wallace's office hours run eight to nine,
and I can't afford to mess up in school this year. Remember
Dr. Bainer? Yeah, he still wants to expel me. I think my
studies were the other reason Kenosha didn't want me
joining their search last night.

I lean back in my comfy black leather chair. Then I take
out my cellphone and call Cat on the off chance that she
answers...

Nope.

This office belongs to my hubby, Professor Bryce
Wallace. But it used to belong to my professor and witch
mentor, Alondra Johansen. We never changed her furniture.
My black leather chair and the fashionable dark mahogany
desk with two red suede chairs belonged to my teacher and

High Priestess of my coven. We also kept her books. I mean, I have a bunch of her books in our home library, once her home library, but there are many very rare esoteric occultist books on the mahogany shelves here in the office.

I grab one of the books I pulled from a shelf, *The Secret Doctrine*, written by Helena Blavatsky. Do you know Helena Blavatsky? Blavatsky was a Russian occultist of the nineteenth century who founded Theosophy. She believed in some pretty crazy stuff, including that the overseer of our world is not God but a demonic demiurge. Or . . . perhaps more accurately, that there is no God. She believed the fall by the serpent represented the fall of the spirit inside man. She spoke of energy, or shakti, in Kundalini descending from the head to the base of our spine. In other words, the snake, or Lucifer, was a positive force sent down for mankind to bring us into consciousness. Hmm...

Kenosha, Mira, and Bryce never found Cat. Well, as Kenosha said, the woods are over a hundred square miles.

Blavatsky, Blavatsky. Come on, Cadence, remember SCHOOL.

When I first met Alondra, she taught me about the thin veneer separating good from evil in our world. I was a shy young student sitting in one of those red suede chairs across from this desk. And she totally intimidated me that morning. Alondra often used fear and mystery to draw us into witchcraft. She was such a wicked witch. I remember her turning a metal pentagram on this desk, flipping good and evil on its head, just like good 'ole Blavatsky.

There's a knock on the door.

"Mrs. Wallace?" a student asks shyly. The threshold reveals a short girl with shaved dark hair, glasses, and a nose ring, with a backpack slung over her shoulder.

"Have a seat," I say with a smile, pointing to the two red chairs.

"I'm Serena."

"Hey, Serena. What's up?"

But then she clams up and keeps quiet for the longest time. She just sits uncomfortably in the red chair with downcast eyes. So I coax her a little. "Dr. Wallace was covering Galen. Is that what you wanted to discuss?"

She quickly shakes her head.

"Good, I was never very good at ancient Roman history."

She laughs.

"Ancient Egypt?" I ask. "Cleopatra? Or is it something in the Middle Ages we've covered, like the Knights Templar?"

"I want to ask about Dr. Alondra Johansen."

"Well, our teacher was renowned, but she's not in the curriculum," I say with a chuckle. "Did you want to borrow one of her books?"

"Word is that Doctor Johansen was an amazing professor," she says. "She was why I chose this class. I grew up in Hawthorne because Dad works in administration, so coming here was easy enough. I get good grades too. I'm a rare Hawthorne native, my family has lived here all my life, Mrs. Wallace. Then, you know, I came to your husband's class because I love secrets and the occult. But—" Serena puts a hand up. "But I'm not here to talk about class. I need to talk to you about something much more important. And I need you to be totally honest with me."

"I hate secrets, Serena."

Her expression turns sour over that.

"Everyone around college knows what you and your friends do," she says carefully. "It's just that, so many are afraid to come out and say it. Even all the other professors. It's like, they're all afraid because they're afraid of you. But I have to talk about it. I need to talk about what you and your friends do outside of class."

Then she forces her eyes on mine. She seems nervous, but very resolute.

"Serena, this is office hours. Other students are probably waiting in the hallway to discuss class. Whatever you're hearing about outside of lecture is really not important for school." She scowls. So . . . I try another angle. "Why do you want to talk about stuff outside of class?"

For some reason, that does it. She puts her head in her hands and starts crying.

"Are you a witch?" she asks, her voice broken up by tears. "You have to tell me. It could mean life or death."

"Yes. I'm a witch. There are plenty of witches in Wicca."

"That's not what I mean," she snaps. "I'm not referring to Wicca."

"There are also practitioners of Thelema. Even Theosophy, which is what I'll be lecturing on next week, is a popular mystic tradition. Many people are practicing witches these days."

"No, I need to know if you cast *real* magic spells, Mrs. Wallace. The whole school heard about your fight with another witch clan a few years ago. There's no proof, but many people saw it. Some videos were on the internet, but taken down. Gossip says the head witch of another clan named Enora turned into a lion and you hurled her across our field near the library. Then there's another story that you were at church and you fought again with Enora and she transformed into black birds and flew off. All the stories point to you fighting this other witch with *real* magic. Some call you the Hawthorne Witch. But—"

Serena stops. She's rubbing her eyes with the backs of her hands, fighting back tears again. I feel horrible. But I can't say anything. If there's one thing Alondra taught me, it was to keep our craft secret.

"Sorry," she says, taking a deep breath.

"It's okay." I reach into a drawer and hand her some tissue. "It's okay. What's this about?"

"Miley. My sister, Miley, is missing. First, she was sick, then, when morning came, Mom started screaming because her bed was left empty. She disappeared. The only hint about where she went was her window was open. She never sleeps with her window open. And our house opens right into the forest."

"Did you tell the police?"

"My sister was taken by magic, Mrs. Wallace," she snaps disdainfully. "The police can't do anything. There was a witch that hurt her and then kidnapped her. If these are just fake stories about you, then . . . then, God, then there's no hope for my sister. That's why I'm not just talking about your *beliefs* in witchcraft. I'm talking about *real magic*. She was taken by witchcraft. I came to ask for your help with magic, not school."

"How do you know a witch took her?"

"The night of Miley's sickness, a witch had come into Hawthorne Sweets and handed out candy canes. All the candy canes turned into insects, but my sister ate one before the transformation. That was the night of her disappearance. My brother, Colton, claims you were in the restaurant at the time."

Oh, *that* Miley.

"*You were there!*" she insists, opening her eyes wide.

"Serena, these are office hours—"

"God, you have to help us!" she says, jumping up. "Please! You're the Hawthorne Witch. Everyone says you are. I told Mom to talk to you, but she doesn't believe in magic, even though she saw the worms too. You have to help my sister!"

There's a knock on the door. That's the next student, or maybe someone checking to see if we're all right because of Serena's yelling.

"You have no idea where she is?" I ask.

"No," Serena says vehemently, shaking her head. "She's been missing for days. I'm so scared."

"I'll do what I can to help get her back."

Serena searches my eyes.

I walk around the desk and put a hand on her back. She surprises me by jumping into my arms.

"I know you will! I just know it! Please. Please! You don't have to tell me a thing about what you and your friends do, just please help Miley. Please. She's such an angel. I can't believe, of all people, this is happening to her."

Then, before I can say another word, she throws open the door and rushes out.

Behind her is a tall boy with glasses, books tucked under an arm, waiting at the threshold. I know this kid from last year's study group. But my cellphone rings in my pants pocket. It's Bryce.

"Just a moment," I say, raising a finger and forcing a smile.

"Katie, come home," Bryce says. "Everyone's here. We're planning to move out this morning with Ray. And Mira says it shouldn't snow or rain, so it'll be easier to do the search."

"She got Miley, Bryce."

"Who's Miley?"

"That little girl I saw talking to Grýla at Hawthorne Sweets. The one who fell sick. God, that crazy witch kidnapped a little girl! Now it's Cat *and* Miley."

"Well, Raymond's here. So is Kenosha and the whole

gang. Everyone is ready to go and search now, but we need our High Priestess. Come home now."

"I'm finishing office hours, babe. There's school too, you know. Kenosha wanted me to cover your office hours—"

"You have to cancel office hours and come home right now, Cadence. Enora's here."

6

———

GRANULATED SUGAR

"Oh, hi Katie." Enora greets me at my front door in a scarlet cloak with her black lace collar. "How are you?"

"What the hell are you doing here, Enora?"

It's not only my archenemy; my whole entryway is full of her scarlet-cloaked goons from her Abaddon coven. Cordelia, Enora's lackey, is stupidly pretending to be offended by my attitude, as usual. You remember that huge bitch. You know, the one with black tattoos covering her face who hung Beatrix a couple years ago in my outdoor patio?

Bryce and Maddie, wearing black robes, rush toward them.

"Katie," Bryce says, "Katie, I let 'em in. Hear them out before you throw them out."

"Well, Cadence," Enora says with her infernal smirk, "seems another maga's decided to attack us from Hawthorne? And it seems, as usual, you don't know what the hell is going on. Well, I'm here to help. I'm always ready for a fight."

"For the last time, I'm not fighting you, Enora."

"I said I'm here to help, Cadence, not fight."

"Everything's prepared outside, High Priestess," Maddie says, out of breath. She hands me a spare black robe. "Willow and Raven have organized the bonfire. Everyone's ready for the meeting."

"You want the Abaddon coven in our backyard, Maddie?" I ask.

"I invited them, Cadence," Bryce replies. "I think Cat needs all the help she can get."

"Yes," Enora replies. "Yes, and we have accepted your Oungan's invitation. But do we have yours, Windstorm?"

"She's never been very respectful, Master." Cordelia is looking down at me with a big smirk.

"You're the one who isn't respectful!" God, as much as I can't stand Enora, I hate Cordelia even more. "All of you villains are outlaws with the council. And most of you belong in prison."

"But if we're going to find our sister Brittany," Enora says solemnly, "seems we need to put our differences aside and work together again."

"Brittany was taken from us in your forest," says a short, quiet witch in a red robe. This witch is a half-shaven blond, like Cat was last year, but with black tattoos—mainly numbers—covering the bald side and her cheek and neck. She looks even younger than Cat. "We're all hurting from this witch, Windstorm."

"Brittany was one of their newest recruits," Bryce explains. "Their youngest. She was only sixteen. Whatever's going on, it's attacking Enora's coven. The search isn't only for Cat and Miley now, it's for their witch too."

"Dream casting is one thing," Enora says. "Kidnapping is quite another. As much as we have our differences, I know you'd never stoop so low as to kidnap one of my sisters, Cadence. This isn't a fight with you."

"Can they join us this morning, Cadence?" Bryce asks.

"Whatever," I say, throwing up my hands.

I make my way around all the red-cloaked bodies and head to our living room. Unfortunately, Enora and her red-robed goons trail me down the main hallway.

"You're showing well," Enora quips, standing behind me. "By the way, I was scrying when you had that blue dream. What a lovely *ville*. I thought the blue was very Kenneth Anger. But the best part was when you were making out with that really handsome man."

I whirl around. The bitch is stupidly smirking.

"Who do you think conjured the cat, Cadence?" she asks. "Might just resolve all the mystery. It wasn't me."

"You can join our meeting, Enora," I say, raising my brow, "but if you get out of line, you and your witches are out of my house. Okay?"

"Sure, Katie," Enora says with a stupid grin. "Sure thing."

My backyard is packed with black cloaks surrounding our central bonfire. White plastic chairs surround the fire, on the wild grass and patches of snow circled by Hawthorne Forest. My coven brought twice as many chairs as usual to accommodate all twelve of our archenemy scarlet-cloaked "friends." None of my black-robed witches look happy to see them. And the bonfire seems super weird under a clear morning sky and bright sun. We never hold ceremony during the day.

Kenosha's already seated. She's wigless, not looking like our dean, but like a forest witch in her green cloak and all these gold necklaces and bracelets. Sitting beside her are Beth, Noori, Abella, Debra, Courtney, Josie, and all the other witches in my coven. Maddie and Bryce approach three open chairs. But then—

"Cadence?"

It's Raymond. Wearing suspenders, he's the only one who looks "normal." The poor guy's eyes are bloodshot.

"I'm so sorry, Raymond," I say, embracing him. "I'm sorry."

"You mind if I join your search?"

I shake my head with a rueful grin, touching his shoulder. He sits down quietly on the opposite side of the fire, near the scarlet-robed witches.

My antebellum house stands behind me. And the forest surrounds us, calming me. All these trees circling the wild grass glade are like a large mother's arms, like blessed Hecate, coming down in one large embrace.

"*Yatu*," I say. I stand and lift my arms before the flames. Quickly, I recite the formal words of ceremony: "Blessed be the day that the circle is brought together. Blessed be the coven under our gods Gaia, Selene, and Astraeus. *Lux alba et tenebris. Atman.*" There, formality's over. "Guys—"

"Glory be the morning star," Enora utters stupidly across from me. Her witches snicker.

"Let's dispense with the formalities, shall we?" Enora asks. "We're meeting with your coven to discuss how we're going to—"

"Cadence is officiating, Enora," Bryce interjects beside me.

"It's okay, Bryce," I object, sitting back down. "It's fine. She's right. I was just about to say we don't have much time."

"Brittany," Enora continues, "was heading back home to meet with us in Atlanta. She and her boyfriend stopped to get gas in your little town. The imbecile said he lost her when he went to pay. He thinks she wandered into your forest. Well, she had a phone. The phone texted me an hour later with the words '*growly, growler.*' Sound familiar? I happen to remember scrying those exact words—"

"You were spying on us again, Enora?" snaps Maddie.

"Hey, don't blame me," Enora says, touching her chest. "Your fake dean is hell bent on arresting me."

"Sooner or later, you'll be imprisoned," Kenosha says. "If it weren't for your lost friend, I would have already called the police."

"Sure, Willow," Enora says, "sure. Anyway, last night, Cadence, you tried your hand at some of my illegal black magic yourself. You used necromancy to scry a cat. Right? And you had that lovely blue dream."

"Keep my business, my business," I warn her, raising my eyebrows.

I glance at Bryce. I haven't told him about my weird dream yet.

"But you summoned a cat, right?" Enora asks. "Just not the daughter of our guest. You summoned a demon cat. What does that tell you? This enemy is attacking you. The witch cast magic in your sleep on your hallowed ground."

"But I'm not sure I was attacked. I'm not as good at divination as you. It could have just been a dream or a botched spell."

"I felt two energies with us last night," Enora says, lifting two fingers. "Two. There was more than just you there. And you don't botch spells. No, there's a new power invading the ether surrounding Hawthorne. Samhain's been pleasantly quiet since we took care of her."

"Katie took care of her," corrects Bryce.

"Sure," continues Enora. "I heard you witnessed a transmutation of candy, Cadence? Apparently, this sick hag likes to tempt kids. Well, guess what? Brittany was our youngest initiate. She's the youngest initiate I've ever let join my coven."

"Beatrix was your youngest witch," snaps Courtney, real

pissed. And Courtney, one of the nicest people I've ever known, looks ready to clobber her. Because Beatrix was killed by Enora's coven, and Beatrix was Courtney's best friend. "I don't think we should let them join us in our search today, Cadence."

"I second that," Mira says.

Enora turns to Raymond, by her side. "How old is your daughter, ghost hunter?"

"Seventeen," says Raymond.

"Twisted bitch is going after kids," Enora says with a shrug. "Look, Courtney, I mustn't be so bad. You would never have married your lover if it weren't for me."

"Shut up, Panthera," snaps Courtney. "*You—*"

"Calm the hell down," Enora says. "Whatever, all right? We're here to help Hawthorne fight this witch. We have to work together. The witch is attacking both our covens."

"Sit down, guys," I say. "Come on." I'm trying to look calm, but honestly I don't totally disagree with Courtney.

"The Abaddon coven shouldn't be here, High Priestess," Courtney repeats.

"We have to help the kids." I turn to Kenosha. "Kenosha, Melanie told Maddie and me that the energy around this season feeds off the young. That might be some hint as to why the children are being abducted."

"This time of the Beldani wheel is one of death," Kenosha says. She turns to my coven's new recruits. "Yule, or Christmas, comes after celebrating the death of the witches' new year in October, Samhain. It's this time of year when everything freezes and dies and the circle is up for renewal. If stuck, the wheel becomes unbalanced, tilting towards lifelessness, and seeks the energy of our youth. This explains the Christmas tale of Grýla in Iceland. Many think Grýla is a myth to explain the deaths of children lost in the snow covered forest. Or, similarly, there's the other Christmas monster, Krampus, that punishes naughty children who stray from their parents' rules and protection. All these myths center around dark energy overpowering the light of the young and innocent during the harsh winter. The greatest power of the sun comes from our young. In fact, some more sinister, dark practitioners try to harness this energy from children."

"Grýla seems to be feeding off this season's energy," I say.

"What does this have to do with Grýla, Cadence?" asks Enora. "Willow just said she's a myth."

"Grýla is the witch who attacked Miley in our ice cream parlor. She called herself Grýla."

"And who the hell's Miley?" Enora snaps. "Cadence, if you want me and my witches to help, you're gonna have to tell me and my coven everything."

"We don't want your help," says Mira.

"Miley is the little girl that's missing with Cat," I say. "She got sick when Grýla turned the candy canes to worms."

"Can you scry this witch, Master?" asks Cordelia.

"I can scry anyone, Adder," replies Enora. "But I can't very well scry a witch I've never seen. Tell me, what does this Grýla look like? Do you have anything of hers? Clothes? Keepsakes? Leftover food? Those candies that turned to worms? Give me an object and I can find her through my black mirror."

"She looks like Mother Shipton," Bryce says. "She's a classic hunched-over old witch in tattered clothes with a long nose and warts. We've seen her rummaging through trash on campus. She's homeless, which fits the Grýla legend. Grýla used to snatch children while she was dressed like a beggar."

"A woman rummaging through trash at Hawthorne

University," Enora says, bursting out laughing, "has kidnapped two witches from our covens? A bum kidnapped Brittany? Come on! You have to be kidding. You guys have this all wrong."

"The woman is possessed by a demon," Kenosha says earnestly.

"You fucking think everybody's possessed by a demon," says Enora. "Look, just show me the bitch and then my witches and I will kill her. Possessed or not. Simple and easy. Right, witches?"

"Yes, Master," say many witches in red, nodding their heads.

"You can't kill her, stupid," Mira says, rolling her eyes. "If it's a possession, the Ekimmu will simply move to another vessel. We need to go after the source."

"Who listens to you, Raven?" asks Enora.

"You're lucky Windstorm is allowing you here in her backyard," Kenosha replies. "I should have called the police."

"Go ahead. Maybe we can waste time casting curses instead of finding our lost kids?"

"You have no business scrying anyone," says Kenosha.

Chandra kicks me. Is she getting riled up by the fight? I hardly blame you, sweetheart. There are few people more irritating than Enora. But I'm kicked again. No . . . it's something else. *What? What is it, Chandra?*

There's a taste of granulated sugar along my lips. I lick my lips again. It tastes so sweet and yummy. It's like someone poured a whole jar of sugar over them. And . . . there's a creamy taste too. Like a wonderful swirl of thick rich chocolate ganache.

Of course, Kenosha, Mira, Courtney, Maddie, Cordelia,

and Enora are now standing and screaming at each other, ready to clobber one another. That's no surprise. The surprise is that they didn't go at it the minute we walked outside.

"Shut up, guys, 'kay?" I say. "Shut up for a second." I stand up and start scanning the trees. "Grýla's casting. Chandra always kicks when I taste sugar."

"But it's your hallowed ground, Cadence," says Maddie, sitting under me, sounding creeped out. "*Stop fighting and shut up, guys!*" Maddie cries. "*Katie's sensing the witch is here right now!*"

That quiets them. Enora pulls out her long thin black wand and searches the woods too. Then Mira, Bryce, and Kenosha search the trees.

"Call your watchers, Cadence," Kenosha suggests, looking everywhere. "Ask them to find her. The witch will lead us to the kids."

I hear cackling. It's a witch's laughter mixed with the sound of babies crying.

"*Coward!*" cries Enora, jumping up. "*Take one of mine? Wait till I get my hands on you!*"

But then everything falls quiet. Too quiet . . .

A wind gently brushes through the wild grass as clouds rush overhead at unnatural speed, at times blocking the sun. Then a few leaves flutter, and some small branches sway. The wind blows harder and trees sway. That's followed by a tempest so strong that it sways some of the tree trunks. Bryce leaps up and holds me just in time before I'm thrown to the ground. Many other witches are knocked down. It's such a powerful gale that it douses our large bonfire. But then . . .

Silence again. It's like, just another clear-skied sunny day.

"Was that one of you?" Enora asks, totally spooked. "Cadence?"

I shake my head, searching the trees.

"I think this witch has more power than just transforming candy, guys," Mira says, standing back up, with her eyes bulging.

I see a shadow running under a tree a few yards away. Is it her? It's too dark to tell. But I think I see white eyes.

"*Goetia!*" I cry. "*Goetia, Goetia, Goetia!*"

My casting is partly a reflex to get Grýla—or whoever it is—out from hiding in the woods. The other part is to follow Kenosha's advice and bring out the dark shadows I control.

Tall dark shades fly from their hiding places in tree branches and behind tree trunks. Darkness occludes the sun above. My friends can't see the demons, but they see a shadow engulfing my glade. And it turns so cold.

Shadows converge over a figure hiding in the trees. I hear wailing. Then the dark figure is consumed in a black, spinning tornado. And she's gone.

And it's quiet again.

"*Lux!*" I cry, raising my arms. The bonfire relights. And the sun shines brightly through clouds above.

"*Nativitatis Maga. Catrina. Show me Catrina! By Hecate, show Cat, Miley, and Brittany's location to the Hawthorne Witch! Reveal yourself to the Hawthorne and Abaddon covens now.*"

But the cackling returns, echoing more loudly in the forest.

"*Bitch!*" Enora cries, swinging her thin wand in the direction of laughter. She strikes her wand against a black book she's clutching at her chest shouting, "*Manifesta Amica! Resurgo. Resurgo. Upon Hawthorne, corvus. Resurgo. Yule Maga! Show yourself! And bring back Brittany! Corvus, corvus, corvus!*"

A rush of caws thunders from the branches of the trees. And then hundreds of black birds swarm out—so many birds fly up into the sky that the sun's rays are blocked out again.

"Between your magic and mine, we'll find her, Windstorm!" Enora cries. "*Come on Abaddon witches. Let's get her!*"

And Enora runs with her red-cloaked witches into the trees.

"Wait, Enora!" I cry. "Wait! Stay here in my backyard with us!"

The sugary taste has left my lips. And Chandra's calming down inside my belly. I think the witch is gone.

"We have to plan this out, guys!" I shout. "*Stop, Enora! Stop! Stop running away!*"

But Enora and her whole red-robed group disappear into a dark fog in the trees. Many of my sisters from my circle—Abella, Josie, Nancy, Beth, and Noori—aren't far behind them. That's followed by cawing and a rush of more ravens.

"*Wait! Stop, guys!*"

7

―――――

GIANT GREEN GUMDROP

SNOWFLAKES SLOWLY FLOAT DOWN, LANDING AS WHITE FLUFF on tree branches, leaves, and our muddy path as I'm walking beside Bryce under a thick forest canopy. It's beautiful when yellow rays of sunlight occasionally break through tree branches. But although it's nearly midday, the fog is thick enough to make it as dark as night. Ever since I summoned demons, it seems darkness has fallen everywhere. My hands are digging in my jeans pockets under my cloak, and Bryce is holding me tightly. Meanwhile our witchy flat black boots keep crunching on ice mixed with leaves and pine needles. But despite all the cold, I still smell that scent of elm and earthy wet mud from the forest I love.

Bryce helps me over a large fallen tree trunk. I have to hand him my old leather-bound grimoire, *Broomstick*, for a second as I lean on my arms, hands in knitted gray gloves pressed against the hard, spiky bark. Then we're back to meandering down the dirt path, covered with patches of snow.

I hear shouting. It's Enora's shrill voice. How can someone so pretty have such an annoying voice? She's so loud, but she's probably miles from here. We've lost her and the others. But I still see her birds. Ravens are everywhere, perched on branches, on ice, or along the muddy path. Some of their small shadows are sweeping from branch to branch above. And yet, aside from blackbird wings fluttering, and Enora barking, it's pretty quiet.

"Do insects freeze when it's icy cold out, Bryce?" I ask. "I always wondered why it seems quieter when it snows."

"Bugs die in the cold, Kate. They just lay eggs."

"Oh, that'd be why," I say with a nod, squeezing him close. "You're so smart."

"I'm your professor. Look, it's been hours and you're getting cold. I'm worried about Cat, but we have to head back soon. Maybe regroup for another search with the others tomorrow?"

"Where'd they all go? It's weird. I thought Maddie and Mira were right behind us?"

"I keep hearing their voices. They haven't strayed that far off."

"Do you even know how to get back?"

"Yes . . ." He stops walking and looks around. "I think so. We've circled a few times. We're not too far from our house."

"Bryce, Cat won't survive another night alone. We have to keep searching. We just have to."

There's another break in the clouds and, for a moment, the entire forest brightens enough for me to have to squint and avert my eyes.

And then I hear whispers.

"Did you hear that?"

He nods. But he doesn't look like he wanted to.

I lift a tree branch from the snow, blow at some moss and leaves at the tip with my frosty breath, and mutter "*lux.*" Then the branch is aflame.

"At least I'm with a powerful witch," Bryce quips.

It's then, under firelight from my makeshift torch, that I find something lying by my black boots on the snowy trail. I kneel for a better look. It's so weird. It's a piece of brown crust with a white center lying in the snow. I try to pick it up, but it's hard to grab anything in these thick snow gloves. Bryce reaches down to help with his bare hands—but then we lurch back when one of Enora's ravens swoops down and snatches it from his hand.

"Shoo!" I say. "Shoo! Go away! Get out of here! God, her stupid birds are everywhere, Bryce! They're as annoying as she is."

"What was that?" Bryce says, staring at our find. "A breadcrumb? Are we supposed to be Hansel and Gretel? Is this witch playing a bad joke?"

I spot another breadcrumb a few yards farther down the path and point at it.

"So, you're Gretel and I'm Hansel, Cadence? I really don't like this. This witch might be nuttier than Melanie."

"Wouldn't know with all of Enora's stupid birds. I think the woods have turned darker with her birds and my spell-casting."

Whispers interrupt our talking again. So this time, I whisper back.

"*Nativitatis Maga. Nativitatis Maga.* By Hecate, reveal yourself to Hawthorne, Yuletide Witch."

"*Cadence! Cadence!*"

Bryce and I spin around in the direction of the shouting. That was Cat's voice! I'm forced to squint as the sun's rays open again through a gap in the trees. But then Cat stops crying for help.

Light shines over our dirt path, winding through the trees, and I see more breadcrumbs strewn along the ground.

I don't follow the path. Instead, I walk off the trail and start gathering large fallen branches in the bushes. I pile the thickest ones and start forming a five-pointed star.

"What are you doing, Katie?" Bryce asks.

"I don't know. I remember doing this in my dream. All this happened before, in the dream...or...I foresaw it happening. You and I first spotted breadcrumbs. So I built this sigil as a signal and as a refuge during the nightmare. I think the headmaster's right, this witch is very powerful. She, or whoever's possessing her, is attacking us with powerful magic. I feel like I have to build this circle for protection."

And I drag another stick along the ice, forming a circle surrounding my pentagram. Then I gesture at my work.

Bryce nods, but then he freaks me out when he covers his eyes, squinting over my left shoulder. Turning in the direction of his gaze, I see a bright golden glow. The light is heralding a small cottage among the trees. The breadcrumb trail ends at a walkway surrounding the cottage, which has two windows with shutters and a chimney. It's as if the cottage has always been there, hidden in the woods. Two large red poles with white stripes by the entrance appear to be the size of people. They look like huge peppermint candy canes. And beside the peppermint sticks, in the snow, are two gingerbread-like statues about half my height. The top of one of the peppermint sticks forms the outline of a girl's face. But her expression is frozen, motionless, like a statue. An icy pathway of shiny red and green candy tiles leads to the front door. The door and the shutters are composed of a brown cake-like substance. Gingerbread? White patches on the walls form a thick plaster. On the plaster brush marks stick out in sections, reminding me of frosting. Soft red and green gems embedded in the white plaster, covered in crystalized sugar kernels, reflect the golden sunlight. Gumdrops or sugar plums. Chocolatey-brown drippings fall from the rooftops, draining into chocolate pools. And the roof is made of a cinnamon red candy–like surface.

We walk slowly along the candy path. Bryce runs a finger along the white plaster beside the door. It's not solid, and it's not plaster, it's like a thick white goo.

"Frosting?" Bryce asks me with a nervous chuckle.

I nod and run my finger along the wall too. I bring the goo to my nose. It smells so sweet and delicious.

"This has to stop," snaps Bryce. "This sick witch is controlling us like in a fairy tale. And . . . I feel drowsy, as if I'm dreaming, Kate. I think she's putting a spell on us."

How can she not be? We're standing in front of a ginger-bread house.

I nab a large crystalized green gumdrop the size of my palm, stuck to the white frosting, and bite into it. It tastes so good! It's soft, full of granules of sugar, with a wonderful tangy sweet lime. And the best part is the consistency. The gob sticks in my mouth like chewing gum.

"Cadence, what are you doing!"

He tries to snatch it from my fingers, but I pull it away. I don't know why I'm eating it, but I am. It's like I'm compelled to eat it. But it tastes sooo good. I don't know how Bryce is stopping himself. I'm so hungry.

"It tastes really good, Bryce," I say with my mouth full. "Wow. You should try some." Then I dip it in some of the wall plaster and offer him some. "Try it, babe. Just take a bite."

"Growly, growler. Growly, growler."

That stops my chomping.

"Cadence, what's going on?"

"Try your phone, Bryce. Try to call the others."

But I lick the uneaten edge of my giant gumdrop. Those crystals seem to pop on my tongue.

"See . . . see if you can reach Kenosha or Mira, Bryce."

But as he reaches for his phone, he touches a red gumdrop fixed to the wall. This one's smaller, about the size of his fingertip. He puts his cellphone back in his pocket and throws the gumdrop in his mouth. All the while, I'm still busy dipping my gumdrop in the frosting, swirling it around to get just the right amount of frosting dip, and then taking more bites out of it. Bryce runs his hand along the soft, sweet glaze covering the wall and starts licking his fingers. Then he bites down on some of my gumdrop.

"Open the door, Bryce," I say, with my mouth still full. "Come on, we have to help the kids."

When he's hesitant, I open the door.

The cottage is made up of only three large rooms. One side, to my right, is the kitchen, another a dining room, and another is some sort of storage room full of large wooden crates. A wooden table spans most of the central room with food piled up over an elegant white tablecloth. Cakes, cupcakes, éclairs, donuts, tiramisu, ice cream dishes, cookies, macaroons, brownies, mixed berry parfait, raspberry, powdered sugar, snickerdoodle cookies, chocolate mousse, pina colada lasagna, chocolate soufflé, and some yummy treats that are covered in chocolate and vanilla swirled frosting.

"Growly, growler. Growly, Growler."

In the kitchen, the mad witch is mumbling those words to herself, crouched over a fiery stove and large black cauldron. The old hag's still wearing the same tatters as in the ice cream parlor—a worn brown cloth dress with a black hood covering her head. She's hunched over, with her back to us, turning a huge wooden spoon in a boiling brew in the cauldron. The cauldron is a couple feet wide.

I hear children crying. But it seems to be coming from inside the walls.

Then I lurch back and gasp as a child's drenched head emerges from Grýla's huge cauldron. A dark-haired boy climbs out of the huge pot with a dripping T-shirt and shorts, as if emerging from a relaxing dip in a Jacuzzi. He walks over to the other side of the cottage, where I saw the stacked boxes. Then the wet boy opens a box and crawls in. He closes a wooden door on himself.

Wait . . . those aren't crates at the opposite side of the house—they're wooden cages. Inside all the cages are children! *And I see Cat!* She's packed like a sardine in one of the small wooden cages with her arms folded around her legs. It seems she can barely fit. I'm not sure why she doesn't just kick the door open. I don't see a lock. Instead of fighting, Cat keeps closing her eyes and sucking on a straw. Some chocolatey goo has fallen all over her neck and stained her white T-shirt.

"Come in, Pappa, come in," Grýla says, stirring her pot, cocking her head back. "Try some treats. Let's see, we have so many treats for children to eats. And for Pappa too. Yes we do, yes we do."

"*Run, Cadence!*" shouts Cat, suddenly opening her eyes wide. "*Run! Get out of here while you can!*"

Grýla whirls around at Cat and shouts, "*Make 'em plump, make 'em strong! So they may run, run, run along!*"

I feel possessed by terrible hunger. I rush to the table and start shuffling éclairs in my mouth. I grab a blueberry parfait. Some of the jelly drips down my lips. I bite into a chocolate donut, dipping it in the chocolate mousse. I smear it all by running the back of my hand over my lips.

"*Leave her alone!*" screams Cat. "*Cadence! No! God, stop her! Please stop her!*"

Grýla bursts into laughter.

Then I hear something scurry behind me. Running by the wall is a large black cat. The black cat bends down, bubbles, and distorts, and then forms into a huge broad-shouldered, dark-skinned man. He is naked. I recognize him as that oaf in my blue dream. His eyes shimmer sapphire. And he's nearly twice the height of Bryce.

"Go, Bryce," I say weakly, gathering a handful of sugar-coated raisins. "Run to the protective circle I made outside."

"Leave?" asks Grýla. "But why? Pappa, why would you leave while the stew's hot? I brew such a nice broth for you two. Mamma and Pappa are my guests. First, try a candy snack before you go. Go ahead. Eat for Chandra. It tastes so sweet and gobbly."

Grýla points to bright red hard candy in a small barrel by the door.

Bryce runs to the door. I'm thinking he's rushing out to get to my circle, but no—he lands on his knees and starts funneling the red candy into his mouth.

"Eat, eat!" storms Grýla, laughing. She hobbles to me. "More and more! Let's see . . . in my pockets, why, what else do I have here for you, child?" She digs in the pockets of her tattered dress. Then she pulls out some things wrapped in plastic. "See, I have fingers and toes, dear. Fingers and toes!"

Inside the plastic, I see fingers and a bloody, torn fingernail.

"Get out, Bryce!" I shout with my mouth full. "Run to my protective circle!"

But Bryce is too weak.

I feel really weak too. And...sleepy. This witch is casting

a spell on us. Last time a witch made me feel this tired, it was Enora fighting me in her lair.

That cat-man grabs Bryce in his huge arms. With one hand, he tears Bryce's shirt off, then he raises Bryce's arms, chaining each wrist to the wall.

"Jola, hand me my athame," Grýla says. "Just more of a taste will pleasure them well enough."

The cat-man hands her a small dagger. Grýla runs dirty fingers with long fingernails along the black handle. Then she runs the silver tip along Bryce's muscular chest and stomach, drawing a line of blood.

"*No!*" I shout. "*You stay away from him!*"

"Handsome, handsome pappa," she remarks.

"*You stay away from him!*" I shout. I raise my grimoire, *Broomstick,* aloft before the witch. "Show your true self. I command you. This is my hallowed ground! *Vade retro demon! Vade retro!* Demon, leave this woman! Leave this vessel!"

The large cat-man disappears. The cabin fades. And for a moment, Grýla looks everywhere around her, disoriented. She puts her head in her hands and shakes it.

But then the house reappears as quickly as it vanished.

"*You have no power here!*" I shout. "*Leave this vessel! I command you, demon. Ekimmu, leave this vessel! The Hawthorne Witch commands you to leave!*"

"*Stop her, Cadence!*" cries Cat.

Grýla licks the blood from the tip of her knife. Then she runs the bloody knife along Bryce's chest again, smearing it red while cackling.

"I'd stop your laughing!" I shout. "There's an army of witches outside searching for the kids. How are you going to defend against all of them?"

"Aren't you pregnant, dear?" the witch asks, turning to

me. Her eyes have turned pearly white. "Feed your baby, feed me. Hungry? Don't worry, your lips be free. Have some more for Chandra. Go ahead. Anything your heart desires in my home. After, when full, the sweetest treat awaits from my pot. Welcome home, child. *My* home be my hallowed ground. Might be your forest, but this be *my* home."

I struggle to keep my eyes open. Bryce's eyes are closed.

Everything blurs. That huge cat-man is back to being a large black cat. It's a Bombay cat, now just brushing his furry back against Bryce's legs.

"And after you have your fill," Grýla says, "sit in the cage by your friend. I have one made for Chandra. Relinquish your book and sit in the cage for your baby. And then . . . guess what? Guess what treat I have for you and your child?"

She takes the book from my hands and I swoon, having difficulty standing.

"What?" I mutter.

"*Milkshakes! Milkshakes!*"

Then the witch guffaws again.

"Now open," Grýla commands. "Open." I lurch back when her wrinkled face and long, crooked nose are right up against my face. Her breath is foul. "Go ahead."

My mouth opens without my control. Grýla throws a handful of orange, green and blue gumballs in my mouth. I chew through the hard shells and the soft centers. It's the sweetest bubble gum I've ever tasted. Then I breathe in a wonderful smell of cinnamon, nutmeg, chocolate, and sugar. And that cornucopia of food on the huge wooden table is under me.

"*Eat, eat,*" she mutters with a nod. "*Navitas Nativitatis. Navitas Nativitatis.* Do you have any idea what I will get out of the sacrifice of you and your unborn child?"

I get on my knees before the table.

"That's it," Grýla cries, bursting into laughter. "*Navitas Nativitatis.* That's it. Eat, drink. Eat to your heart's content. Then vomit it all up. Throw it all up. Then eat more. Upon Saturnalia, eat and eat. And then have more and more and more. *More and more and more!*"

With my teeth, I pick up two large nutty almond brownies with thick fudge frosting. Crumbling it, smearing the chocolate all over my nose and cheeks, I take it all into my mouth. As I swirl the chocolate and run my tongue along my lips and cheeks, I hear crying. Cat's weeping.

Another head bobs up from the water in Grýla's pot. It's Miley! Her long blond hair is drenched. But she doesn't appear to be in pain. She seems to be in a trance, soaking in a gentle pool or sauna.

I dig my face back into the brownies.

"Growly, Growler. Growly, Growler."

8

COTTON CANDY

In a scarlet haze, I follow a winding path through a dark, rocky cave. A pleasant breeze blows along my cheeks carrying sugary whiffs of strawberry and cherry. After I turn a corner, the haze turns dark violet and the smell changes to blueberry. And yet there's a hint of a lovelier sweetness. It's from a stairway cut into the stone painted a slick nutty brown, as if made of chocolate. I'm holding a single dim black candle. And under my rotund stomach, my tanned bare feet look so dark as my toes pass over white flour. It's cold. I shiver. I bring the candle up to my lips to blow it out. Then I take a bite out of the hot candle stalk. It tastes like hot, melting black licorice. And as I slowly meander over white flour, it feels cold as ice, but as white and fluffy as cotton candy.

9

SCRYING FOR WITCHES

"The sun's dropping, it's cold, and we're getting nowhere fast," Enora grumbles, cocking her head back at Maddie and Mira while clutching her arms tightly around her scarlet cloak. "We've been walking for hours."

"And you're complaining as usual," Mira mutters under her breath, rolling her eyes. She's walking behind Enora with Maddie.

"*Revelare*," Enora cries. "*Revelare*. Reveal yourself, witch! Where the hell are you! How long do we have to search this forest for you, coward?"

"Katie could have planned our search if you hadn't run off," Maddie says.

Mira halts. Then she crouches by a tree, closes her eyes, and cups her hand, scooping some soft dirt under the trunk. Here, under the canopy, this is one of the only dry spots. A raven swoops and lands on her shoulder, and she opens her eyes, annoyed, brushing it off. She sniffs the dirt on her palm, letting the sand kernels drift between her fingers.

"We need to find the girls before sunset," Mira says, standing up. "It would be nice if you called off your stupid birds, Enora. As usual, you're fighting against everyone and everything."

Enora's cellphone rings under her red cloak. She reaches into a pocket in her pants.

"Yeah?" Enora says, cradling her phone over her shoulder.

"Thought you didn't believe in using phones?" Maddie quips.

Enora shows Maddie her middle finger.

"Cordelia, where are you?" Enora asks. "Huh? Well, you'll never guess who's with me right now."

Mira surveys the woods. Then she crouches down and steadies her breath, closing her eyes again.

"Bryce and Cadence are still missing," Maddie says almost in a whisper, crouching beside her. "I called but she won't answer her phone. Why? Is it all these clouds and fog mucking up the reception? It's never stopped the signal before. I've never not been able to reach her out here."

"Breadcrumbs?" Enora asks in her phone, laughing. "Breadcrumbs? What the hell are you saying, Adder?" She stupidly laughs harder than ever. "What are you smoking? You're seeing breadcrumbs in the snow? Either you've gone looney or it's our Christmas witch."

"Anything, Meer?" Maddie whispers, laying a hand on her back.

"No, Maddie," Mira says, shaking her head. "Afraid not."

Enora stuffs her phone back in her pocket.

"They've found nothing," Enora says. "Nothing but a stupid trail of breadcrumbs. Twisted Christmas-bitch thinks we're in a goddamn fairy tale. Wait till I meet her and she tries offering me candy."

"Wait, Maddie, look over there!" Mira says. She's

pointing to a bunch of sticks on the ground in a small snowy clearing among the trees. "This looks fresh."

"Mira? Madison?" cries Kenosha's voice.

Kenosha emerges from between two trees in her long forest green robe. Following her is a large group of black robes and Raymond.

"*Yatu*, Raven," Kenosha says, approaching. "Have you found Cadence?"

"Look," Mira says, still staring down. "It's fresh, Willow. But I'm not sure why it's here."

"Didn't Cadence say she made a pentacle, in her dream, to protect her a couple days ago?" asks Kenosha, staring at the find. "Maybe she built a real one to let us know where she is."

"Come on," Enora says, "you guys probably make symbols here all the time."

"Why would High Priestess make a pentagram, Doctor Trent?" asks Beth. Our other new recruits, Nancy and Noori, look over too.

"It's a pentacle, Beth," corrects Kenosha. "A pentacle is a pentagram in a circle. See the circle in the snow around it? Both the pentagram and pentacle are powerful sigils. They can be used for protection. Remember what your daughter, Cat, asked during the séance, Raymond? She asked if we should run a circle of salt around our séance table. Well, during ceremony, sometimes we chalk a circle around our bonfire. This small circle is an area of protection. The pentacle was first used by Babylonians to cast apotropaic spells. Like a lucky charm or a cross warding off a vampire."

"You think Cadence formed this for protection?" Maddie asks.

"Or as a beacon," Kenosha suggests. "And you, felon?"

asks Kenosha, turning to Enora. "Have your sisters found anything?"

"Just breadcrumbs," Enora replies with a smirk.

"I'm getting really worried about Cadence," Maddie says. "She's still missing, Kenosha."

Then Maddie turns and looks right at me.

I'm right here, Maddie! Don't you see me? Right here!

All the other witches lean over the snow, studying my symbol on the ground. But Maddie is still staring in my direction.

She furrows her brow. Then her eyes open wide.

"She's here, guys," Maddie says. She tugs at Mira's arm and points in my direction. "Cadence is right there."

You can see me?

"How do you know, Maddie?" asks Mira. "I don't see a thing."

"I see her," Maddie replies, staring. "I mean . . . I don't see her . . . I sense her. Or I feel her, I think."

"You're staring at trees," Enora quips.

I can't seem to show the rest of them. I don't even know how Maddie's seeing me. We've all thought my best friend has empathic powers.

My knees throb. I'm bent like a pretzel so tightly in this small wooden cage. There's a long straw around my neck running past my cheek. It's full of this really yummy peppermint stick, caramel, and chocolate shake, and I keep feeling compelled to suck it. My heart's racing. And I have a constant ache of hunger.

If I could make enough noise, maybe more of my friends would hear? Or perhaps I could directly talk to Maddie through magical telepathy?

Cat's trapped beside me. She's been whimpering. There are no locks. It's this horrible witch's magic keeping us caged. Cat's face is so messy from spilling that same nasty, wonderful-tasting stuff from a plastic straw. Other kids are in traps below us. They're drinking the chocolate shake poison too.

I stare forward using all my magical intent to see through the wall again. But then I'm too distracted by what's chained before me. Bryce. His eyes are closed, but he keeps wincing in pain. Blood still covers his chest where he was cut by that dagger, but it's dried. And running along his legs is that black demon cat.

I jump. Grýla appears crouched down beside me, opening one of the cages. She yanks out a little blond-haired girl. Miley! The poor little girl is screaming.

"*No! No!*"

"Back in the pot, little one," Grýla says. "Come on. Back inside. Come, come. Back in the water. With all your friends outside, I need you to take a dip for just another small, sweet taste of your lovely baby skin. Or, maybe, maybe, just maybe...*a little more?*" She laughs. "Maybe...a finger or a toe?"

"*Leave her alone!*" screams Cat. "My God! Cadence! Cadence, open your eyes! She's going to hurt Miley!"

"*Shut up!*" Grýla says. "If I hear any more crying from you, I'll do more than use her as stock for my soup, I'll serve you as my main course! You whine too much. You're naughtier than the rest. Even more than this sweet, sweet baby child." Grýla smiles down at Miley. "Now come on, my little sweetness. Back in the pot for another lovely dip."

"*No!*" Miley says, crying. "*I won't! I won't! Leave me alone!*"

Cat kicks her trap open. She charges at Grýla and tugs at Miley's arm.

"*Let her go!*"

"*Let go of me or I'll baste you!*"

"*Let her go!*" Cat screams. "*Let her go!*" Then she turns to me. "*Cadence! Cadence! Open your eyes. You have to help us!*"

I didn't realize my eyes were shut.

"*Stop it!*" cries Miley. "*Stop! Please, please just leave me alone!*"

The little girl's cries are enough to jar me awake.

"She's in trouble," Maddie says.

For a flash, I see all the witches staring in my direction, seeming to finally notice me. And now more scarlet robes are arriving in the woods just in time. There must be thirty witches surrounding Grýla's cottage.

"She's in that weird gingerbread house," Maddie says, pointing again.

"Gingerbread house?" Enora asks scornfully.

"Where do you see her, Maddie?" asks Kenosha.

"Maddie," I say in a forceful whisper. "Maddie, Grýla's going to hurt Miley! You're right, I'm right in front of you. You all have to help us. Quick! You have to go through the front door of the house now!"

But Maddie squints, looking unsure.

"*Goetia,*" I utter. It's barely audible. But Grýla hears, turning.

For a moment, the walls disappear. The wooden cages, the large table, and the cornucopia of food disappear.

Grýla loses her grip on Miley, and the little girl bursts through the door and runs to the group of witches. Beth and Nancy grab her and step in front of her to protect her.

"*Goetia!*" I cry. I feel empowered again. "*Goetia!*"

I burst open my cage door.

"*Goetia! Goetia! Goetia!*"

The cabin disappears.

We're in a glade in the forest again. I look up and the moon and stars keep getting blocked by fluttering shadows.

My devils. And surrounding the flying shadows are soaring black birds.

My friends finally see me. All of them, not just Maddie —the whole group of red- and black-robed witches are staring at us.

But it turns darker than night. And then I shudder as Grýla faces me. The old hag's eyes have turned a creepy pearly white again. And all the darkness, all my shadows, the dark magic, rush behind her. She grows twice her size. And standing beside her is that burly cat monster.

10

—————

WALPURGIS

I'm sitting at my booth in Hawthorne Sweets. This is the same booth I've sat in over the past week, but the restaurant is empty. It's dark with all those red and green Christmas lights switched off. Actually all the lights are out. That's odd. There's only a flickering yellow-and-red flame to my right.

Outside, through the window, naked women circle a large bonfire in the center of the narrow street. Some raise their arms to the sky, some hunch back and shake, but all are smiling and laughing. A few have their eyes wide open, staring, seemingly in madness. I recall my coven disrobing years ago and dancing like this under the power of mandrake or nightshade. But these nude witches are on a narrow street only a half mile from the university.

I realize I'm holding up a silver spoon matching the silver table, but there's no ice cream bowl. And there's hardly any silver on the table surface. The table is a mess, covered with mounds of spilled and melting dark chocolate ice cream.

A huge black bird leaps on the chocolatey goo, fluttering

its wings and splashing some of it at my face. Then it dips its beak down over some of the melted ice cream. Before I can shoo the bird away, it flutters its wings again, spattering me some more. Then it darts off to my left.

The raven soars from the restaurant into a valley. That's so weird because, to my left, there should be a counter for fixing all the ice cream treats. But the wall on my left is gone.

In a valley of charred black dirt, thousands of naked people sit in rows, holding their knees as if in fetal position, the way we sat in Grýla's cages. Their skin is caked in dust and mud, like the Samhain Witch once was. Thousands sit in nearly perfect rows as if someone has gathered inmates or criminals and lined them up. They're the only thing present in the charred valley, except black hills on the far horizon. It's like a volcano with the only living things being the muddy people. It even smells of sulfur.

"They never stop their crying. Never ever."

I'd know that voice anywhere. It's Melanie! But across from me in the booth isn't the Melanie I saw in Savannah. Like the figures lined up in the valley, she's appearing as she once was—a muddy monster, naked, a thin-haired, filthy hag. A thin black snake slithers slowly along her neck. Her eyes are white amidst the mud, and her lips, curled in a smile, are cracked and gray. This is the Melanie I remember from when she was my archenemy—when she once tried to kill me. She looks terrifying.

"I told you, Cadence. They cry and cry and cry. That's what all people do." Although she looks hideous, it's the same normal voice, with a southern accent, I remember from Savannah. She glances at the valley. Then she shakes her head, looking down at the chocolaty mess on the table. "But I sure don't like ice cream."

"What's going on, Melanie? Are you conjuring this place?"

"Why would I do that? I don't like ice cream."

"What's happening? Why are we here?"

"Samhain sure don't like Christmas either," Melanie says, shaking her head. "All that red and green color is so fake. There's no hollies growing on top of chocolate or strawberry ice cream, I tell you."

"How can you help my friends?"

"Seems you're the one who needs help," Melanie says, staring out the window. "Seems things aren't going so well right now in Hawthorne. I thought they weren't. You know, witches cry and cry and cry, Cadence. You all need to just shut your goddamn mouths. That's what I told Bonnie. I said to Bonnie, 'We'd all get along so much better in this world if half the whole world would just stop all their scrying.'"

Her madness is too much for me. I bury my head in my hands. How could she not be conjuring all this?

"Ever wonder why it's dark?" she asks, leaning forward. "Wonder why we travel through mazes come Christmas? Dark to left, fire to right; light candles, incense, upon bonfire light? *Lux Tenebris. Lux alba. Walpurgis. Walpurgis. Walpurgis.* Burn the witch. 'Burn 'em all.' Stop all the magic. And please, please, don't bring me back, Momma."

"What are you saying!" I snap. "Melanie, you have to help me! Just tell me what the hell's going on! Why am I here?"

She leaps over the table and grabs my arm. Her muddy fingers and long fingernails stab my wrist. I remember those sharp nails cutting my neck when she once tried to choke me to death.

"Stop it, Melanie! Stop it. They're trying to help you!"

Then she lets go of my arm and lands back in the booth. She crosses her arms. And then she just stares back at me.

I turn to my left and see that horrible dark valley again. It's like thousands of people suffering in hell. That makes me turn to my right—which is just as bad. There, naked witches keep lifting their arms, shaking their hips, and bouncing their breasts in drug-filled ecstasy. I have nowhere to turn.

"You sacrificed your life for me once, Cadence. So I came to sacrifice for you. Think Samhain wants to be casting again?" She wags a finger. "Stop your crying. I came here to cast magic for you. I sure don't like witches and I don't like ice cream, but Samhain came to help. Now tell her . . . why Walpurgis? Why do witches dance around flames come Walpurgis Night, Cadence Hawthorne?"

And then she just sits with folded arms and waits again. This filthy monster stares at me waiting for an answer, as if she's some wise man asking me to solve a riddle. If I weren't totally freaked out, perhaps it'd be funny.

When I don't answer, she even lifts her mud-caked brow.

"Walpurgis?" I ask. "Walpurgis night, Melanie? You're asking me about Walpurgis?"

"Walpurgis," she echoes with a nod. "Why do witches practice black sabbaths worshipping the devil beside fire, Cadence? Who do they worship under the light of the moon. Selene? Diana? Why do they dance around fire and moonlight? Why do all those sinful, terrible, wicked witches do that? Why did your teacher teach you to say *lux alba* when all that nasty witch ever did in her life was cast evil?"

But I put my head in my hands again, fighting back more tears. Maybe all this magic is a figment of my imagination? Including you. Maybe I'm just losing my mind, about to be killed by Grýla?

When I look up at Melanie, across from me, she's changed. She has pretty long blond hair, like when Maddie and I visited her at her house in Savannah. And she's wearing a lovely long draping saffron dress. She's giving me a gentle smile.

"Burn the witches," Melanie says gently with a nod. "*Walpurgis night,* Cadence. *Walpurgis. Walpurgis. Walpurgis.* You never saw this wicked witch dare show up in Samhain, did you? When there's imbalance, a witch casts a circle. Ouroboros. Snake. Your heart gets it. You cast one before entering her house. Now tell your mind. When Christmas comes all dark, when everything's dying in the snow from the cold, and all the crops wither and decay—people be dying too—what do all the folks celebrating Santa Claus do? Why all these stupid fake red and green lights? And all their children running to see Santa Claus with smiles? What are they smiling about? The cold snow? Their dead, decaying bodies? Their newest gold earrings or pressed pretty dress?" She shakes her head. "They turn darkness to light. They complete the circle of life."

She gestures to the dancers out our window.

"Why do you, Alondra, and Abigail light your candles by your chest? See them dancers? Why are witches always lighting fire in the darkest night, Hawthorne Witch? They dance around fire under moonlight. Moonlight, Windstorm. Selene. Diana. *Lux alba et tenebris*, my dear, sweet friend.

"But if you throw too much chocolate ice cream on the table, what do you get?" She gestures at the table. "A big fucking mess, if you ask me. Don't drag me back into this, Hassyhorn. I told you and Maddie back home that I don't like witches, and I sure don't like ice cream. I don't want to come down and cast magic ever again. Yule's been here ever since I learned witchcraft, but she could never tempt me or

Alondra. Because Samhain sure loved her magic and Alondra—" She chuckles. "Alondra loved herself. This witch can't trap you when you love something more than her temptations."

"I think I suggested this to Bryce," I mutter. "You're telling me Enora and I are empowering this witch with our dark magic? We're making her more powerful with dark necromancy. We're making her possession worse. We need to use light, not darkness to balance Hawthorne."

"Blessed be," she says, nodding and smiling. "You understand?"

"Yes, I think I do. Thank you."

I collect my thoughts, as my teacher once taught me. In deep concentration, I dip my head down and recite aloud:

"White light. Alba. Alba. Bring fire to reveal shadows. Darkness to light. Shadows to fire. Left to right. As below, so above. As above, so below. Reveal my shadows. Shine light upon her daemons and free her."

"Now you're getting it!" Melanie exclaims.

The red and green lights streamed along the restaurant walls switch on. Then come all the lights in the restaurant. The dead valley to my left vanishes. That waitress with the red Santa hat with a white pom-pom appears behind the ice cream counter, and it feels bright and warm. The chocolate ice cream smeared on my table disappears. And outside I see daylight with a normal view of the narrow road that heads to campus.

"Merry Christmas, Cadence," Melanie says, standing up in her long flowing golden dress. The dress matches her long blond hair. This once hideous, filthy witch now seems clean and beautiful with her flowing hair and soft skin. "Won't you come visit me with Madison in Savannah again?

Friday is game night. They're not always serving bologna sandwiches, you know."

11

CLEAN UP MY MESS

I AWAKEN TO A GROWL. THAT MAKES ME MORE DISORIENTED than ever because it sounded like a lion in the forest. *Hawthorne Forest*. What the hell's a lion doing in my forest? A rush of yellow shoots through bushes and leaves, lunging at something in a grassy opening in the trees. It's a huge lion with a mane clawing at the old hag, Grýla! I'm not sure what looks more bizarre—a huge lion in snowy Hawthorne Forest or the old hag, twice her normal size, wrestling one. And it's not only the lion—ravens keep swooping down and pecking at the old witch too. A large group of black- and red-robed spectators are surrounding the fight, keeping their distance.

I'm leaning on my side in that pentacle of branches I designed. It's still dark. Even though the sun's rays keep trying to peek through the thick mist, it's dark as night. Hidden farther behind more trees, Kenosha and three witches in black robes, Nancy, Josie, and Beth, are standing in front of Miley, protecting her.

"Katie," says Maddie, crouching over me. "Katie, wake up."

"Cadence, are you all right?" asks Bryce. "We brought you inside the circle."

Seeing Bryce energizes me. He's not chained. He's even wearing his shirt and holding my book, *Broomstick*, under his arm.

"Where are the kids?" I ask with a nod. "Where's Cat?"

"There were more kids in the house?" Maddie asks. "Only this little girl ran out before it disappeared. We haven't seen Cat or any other kid. Only that horrible witch."

There's another growl.

"*Laugh in your grave!*" shouts a guttural voice.

That's Enora. She's talking as a lion, just like she did once while fighting me on campus. Enora *is* the lion. Grýla hurls her twenty yards into a tree trunk, splintering the tree. But the minute Grýla stands tall, a flock of ravens pounce on her. The lion growls, its sound echoing in the woods. Then she charges the witch, knocking her down and rolling with her again.

"We need to find the kids," I say, reaching for my friends to help me up. "We have to help them."

There's a yelp as the lion is thrown across the field into another tree. Then a large black cat the size of a panther leaps from the shadows and pounces on her. As more ravens crowd Grýla, the lion wrestles the large black cat.

I snatch my book from Bryce and walk out of my magic circle.

"Cadence, take it easy," warns Bryce. "Be careful!"

"*Manifesta*," I say, raising my arms toward the lion. "*Manifesta! Manifesta Enora.*"

As the lion lunges for the black cat, Enora's transformed back into her human form in midair. Enora rolls away on the grass just in time to miss the black cat's teeth.

"*Igni!*" Mira shouts, holding her grimoire over the cat. "*Igni!*"

The black cat catches on fire. Then a swarm of red-robed witches quickly drag Enora out of the animal's reach.

Grýla isn't fighting her birds anymore. All of Enora's black birds are lying in the grass, shaking and twitching in a circle around the hag.

Enora pulls out her wand.

"Enora!" I shout. "Stop!" I reach out my hand and will her wand to fly out of her grasp. "Stop casting black magic! Our dark magic is empowering the witch!"

"Whose side are you on!" cries Cordelia. "Fighting against Master again?" Many other red-robed witches shout at me.

"You have to stop fighting with dark magic, guys!" I yell. I look up at the darkness above. "Away, daemons! Away! By Hecate, I call off this attack. And I call off Enora's magic upon my hallowed ground!"

My shadows disperse, freeing the sky. Bright rays from the sun make me squint, warming my face and brightening the whole forest. And then, Melanie's right. Grýla shrinks back to her normal height. And that beastly huge black cat turns back into a small Bombay cat, now smoking and rolling on the ground, dousing Mira's fire spell.

I'm viciously slugged in the face. *Oww!* I'm clutching my cheek and jaw as I fall to the ground. Shit, that hurt! *Oww!* Then, the infernal gargantuan tattooed-face bitch, Cordelia, jumps on top of me, crashing her fists against my face and chest. Bryce mercifully tears her off me.

"Stand down, Adder!" shouts Enora. "Okay, Katie, okay, if you've got some trick under your sleeve, do it now!"

"Where's Cat!" I shout at Grýla. "Where's Brittany? Where are all the children!"

Grýla straightens, staring at me with her creepy white eyes, brushes off the dirt, and leaves. "Is *Chandra* hungry?"

"Reveal your name, demon!" I shout. With both hands, I lift *Broomstick* before me again. "By the power upon this hallowed ground, *my* Hawthorne, I ask you to reveal your real name. This land might be your grounds, but this entire forest is mine. *Tell us your name. I command you!*"

"*Behemah*," whispers the forest, "*Behemah, Behemah.*"

But Grýla says nothing, crouched down facing me, just creepily staring with her pearly-white eyes.

I wipe dampness from my face, where Cordelia hit me, expecting the salty taste of blood. But . . . my lips taste weird. There's this strange mix of honey and marshmallow as I chew on something soft. It's . . . it's a . . . candy corn taste. Chandra is doing somersaults in my belly. Ever since I was a child, candy corn has been one of my favorite treats on Halloween. Apparently she likes it too. Images of bags of candy corn I ate as a child flood my mind. There was a special taste to the candy back then. You know, the taste of food changes over time. I'm not sure if it's our memory of the food, or if it's the manufacturer changing the recipe, but food never tastes as good as it once did. Well, the taste of this candy corn is amazing. It tastes like the candy corn in the bag I stole from Damie when I was seven.

More sunlight glows on the base of a tree trunk, as if a floodlight is shining, illuminating a pile of candy corn.

I fall to the ground and crawl toward the tree trunk.

No, Chandra, no . . .

"Back in your cage," Grýla says, laughing. "Get back now, dear *Chandra*, so that you and Momma may have your fill of all my tasty treats."

A flash of light blinds me. Grýla screams. My eyes burn. And then my ears ring. That was my magical thunderbolt.

My windstorm. I didn't hit her directly. I mean . . . I don't want to kill her; I want to exorcise her demon.

For a moment, sitting on the snowy grass, Grýla brings her face to her hands, shaking her head. Her wrath fades and she looks confused.

More thunder is heard under a cloudless sky.

"She's still tempting me with Chandra!" I cry, looking back at Enora and Kenosha. "I need help, guys. I don't think I can stop her without killing her! Willow, you and both Ravens can try. You three witches love magic more than anything else. You three can try to fight off her magic."

Grýla stands up. So I focus my intent and ready another lightning strike.

"Stay back!"

Grýla's creepy eyes glow a brighter white.

I have to save the kids. I just have to!

Don't you worry, I know what to do.

I quickly scuttle over on all fours to the tree trunk. I cup my hands and funnel as much of the candy corn into my mouth as I can. My baby dances in my belly again. I figure the more candy I eat, the more satisfied I'll be, and the easier it will be to fight her. Right? And that . . . honey-and-sugar taste is *so, so* sweet. Babies cry again. Or is that Cat?

Desperate, I recite the Lord's Prayer.

Then I shuffle more candy pieces in my mouth, licking and relishing the honey-sweet taste.

"*Exi seductor, Behemah!*" cry Mira, Kenosha and Enora in unison. Their voices echo in the woods. "*Behemah, leave this vessel. Behemah! Exi! Exi! Exi!*"

12

MARGARET

I HEAR THE SOUND OF CRYING. THIS TIME, IT'S NOT A BABY crying—it's a group of children. A dozen kids are standing in a circle in the trees, back where the cottage materialized, sobbing. The cottage is gone. All the witches, in black and red, are crouched down trying to comfort them. Raymond has Cat in his embrace.

I'm standing beside Bryce. He's holding me, but I feel so weak. The trees are spinning. I squint up at the sun; it's so bright above me in a clear sky. I love the warmth on my face —this bright light that Melanie suggested I conjure to stop the witch.

No, not my conjuring, it's always there. I simply removed my spell.

"Cadence?" asks Bryce.

I nod. But I can't stop shaking.

"We have to go home," Bryce says quietly, rubbing my arms and back. "You're shivering and the sun's falling."

"It's not just the cold. I'm still weak, Bryce."

"It's over, Cadence," says Cat, next to her dad. She jumps

into my arms. "You did it. Thank you! You saved me. All the witches did. They fought her and her spell is over."

"Where is she, Cat?" I ask "Where's Grýla?"

"Not Grýla," Cat says with a smile, pointing. "Margaret."

Cat points to three witches—one in scarlet, two in black —huddled over an old lady in rags. It's Enora, Kenosha, and Mira. The old lady is sitting under them stroking the black fur of a Bombay cat in her arms.

"Margaret?" I ask, standing over the old lady.

Margaret just looks up, confused.

"She doesn't remember a thing, Cadence," Mira says, looking up from where she is huddling beside Margaret. "We're trying to help her, but she's so confused. She doesn't even know why we're in the forest."

Enora's surprised by a young lady with smeared black makeup barreling into her arms. Brittany, I presume?

"Well, Cadence," Enora says, holding Brittany. "Glad we didn't fight each other. I figured when you act your strangest, you're on to something."

"Thanks . . . I guess."

"Bye, my Amica. Send love and kisses to Willow."

"And where do you think you're going, Enora?" Kenosha asks, looking up from Margaret.

"I'm going to live happily ever after worshipping Satan in Atlanta," Enora says, putting an arm around Brittany and walking with her. "Bye bye." And all the red-robed witches of her Abaddon coven walk off with her. Brittany is still in Enora's arms, crying, as Enora says, with her back turned, "Till we meet again, Hawthorne witches."

"I really can't stand her," Maddie says. She's got that right. Then my face aches so bad. I'm suddenly reminded of her henchwoman Cordelia's vicious pummeling.

"Let's go home, Cadence," Bryce says.

But Kenosha is still crouched over Margaret. And Margaret is just petting her furry black cat, who is in her arms.

"Is there anything we can do for her, Kenosha?" Maddie asks.

"I'm hungry," Margaret says, looking up at me.

13

TOTALLY SANTA

"Wait a second, guys. Slow down. Don't open all your gifts at once. Ever since I was little, Damie and I have gone around the room passing out gifts and watching each person open their present one at a time."

"But that was just you and me, sis," my brother Damie says. "It's gonna take all night for the whole coven."

Damie's got a point there. There are like twenty of my friends packed in my living room—so many that a few people have to stand by the doorway. I even hear a few of my witches hanging out in the kitchen.

It's kind of fun to see my witches in festive Christmas clothes. Damien has on a corny red sweater and Maddie, beside him, is in a red V-necked T-shirt with a snowman. My hubby is standing beside me, close to our red and green Christmas tree, wearing a nice black short-sleeved button-down. He's enjoying some spiked egg nog he made (wish I could try it. No alcohol for you, sweetheart). Mira and Courtney are across from us on the sofa. I don't have to tell you what Mira's wearing, do I? The only time I ever saw Mira not wear black was at Dad's wedding. She's in a black dress. All the rest of the newbie witches are decking the halls too. Besties Beth and Nancy are with Gail and Noori, sitting on the floor around the sofa. Abella's cross-legged on the carpet. She chose the same witchy attire as Mira. All my friends in my circle are here for my Christmas Day get together.

"Okay, Cadence," Mira says, holding a large red box with a green ribbon. "Who first then?"

"Me."

We laugh.

"Just kidding," I say. "How about our dean?"

"That's okay, Cadence," Kenosha says dismissively, sitting by the sliding glass door. She's wigless in a lovely green dress.

I shake my head and move to stand up, but then I nearly fall. Cat and Raymond jump up to help me. Geesh, Chandra, are you getting so big that I can't rise? I reach down and grab a small, heavy violet felt box wrapped in a green bow under the tree and hand it to her with a smile.

"What's this?" asks Kenosha with a smile. She bounces it in her hand. "It feels heavy. You didn't have to get me a thing, Windstorm."

"Merry Christmas, Kenosha," I say, shaking my head. "It's from me and Bryce."

"Happy Yule," Kenosha says with a nod.

I turn to Bryce. He winks.

Kenosha pulls off the bow and opens the box, revealing a small crystal ball. It's not perfectly smooth, it has cracks in it. But all the red and green lights from my tree are so pretty reflected in it.

"I owed you a new one," I say.

She lifts it, bouncing the crystal and weighing it in her palm.

"I can't accept this," Kenosha says, staring at it. "This must be so expensive. This is real quartz, right? How could you and Bryce afford this?"

"We found it in a cabinet in Alondra's library upstairs," Bryce says. "I suppose, if you want, you could bring it back to Clotho to replace the one Katie broke in your coven in New Orleans?"

"Or just keep it for yourself," I say.

She doesn't look like she's returning anything. She can't stop staring into the sparkly glass. Kenosha reaches up for a hug, and Bryce and I dip down and embrace her.

Then shy Nancy opens a small box, revealing earrings. Bryce opens a box from me of his favorite cologne. And then all descends into chaos. Everybody's opening presents around me. *Oh, well.*

"Looks like we're just opening everything now," says Cat beside me with a grin. "Can I open mine?"

"Sure, go ahead, Cat," I say with a sigh.

There goes order. But, you know, everyone's smiling and looking so happy and I suppose that's all that really matters.

"Listen, guys," I say. But everybody's too busy opening presents. "Listen."

"Hey, everyone," Maddie shouts. "Everyone shut up! Cadence wants to say something."

"*Shut up!*" shouts Mira. "Go ahead, Cadence." Mira always knew how to clear a room.

But then everyone's staring at me. Some are midway through tearing off red and green wrapping paper.

"I . . . " Geesh, *everybody's* looking at me. "I just wanted to thank all of you for coming on Bryce's and my invitation. I love you all so much. No matter what happens in Hawthorne, it's always been about us. About our friendship and being together, you know. Just . . . Merry Christmas everyone."

"Merry Christmas!" shouts everyone.

Maddie smiles and nods. Then Damie finishes opening his gift beside her, completely oblivious. It's all right, we love him.

Bryce jumps up from the carpet and kisses my cheek.

"We all love you, Cadence," says Bryce.

"Hi, kids," says somebody walking into the living room. It's Aunt Jane and Dad. "Bryce. Cadence. We have a special surprise for you. Look who we brought along." And Aunt Jane gestures to a blond woman trailing her and Dad, looking like her twin, only about twenty years younger.

It's Melanie. She looks coy, nodding to everyone and smiling but not meeting anyone's gaze. Many in the room aren't smiling. Kenosha, for one, just lost all her joy.

"Hi," Melanie says, waving a hand. Both she and Aunt Jane are wearing lovely green dresses. I wonder if Melanie's dress was Aunt Jane's?

"Hi, Melanie," Maddie says. She walks over and hugs her. "I'm so glad you could come."

"Cadence invited me," she says, smiling at me.

"Hi, Melanie," I say. "Welcome." I walk over and hug her too. Then I hug Aunt Jane and Dad.

"Sure is cold outside," Melanie says to me. Aunt Jane helps her sit down on a plastic chair near the couch. "But it's nice and warm in Windstorm's house. Hi, Bryce. Good to be having ceremony with your witch circle indoors, where it's warm, this evening."

"This isn't a witch ceremony," Damie says.

"Welcome, Melanie," I repeat. Then I turn to Damie and quickly shake my head, shushing him.

"One gift at a time and everybody watches as we unwrap it," I repeat, heading back to my chair. "Okay?"

"Who next then, High Priestess?" asks Nancy.

"How 'bout you?"

"Let Mira go," Courtney says. "She's been holding it forever."

We all laugh. Mira rolls her eyes.

"Happy Yule, Meer," Courtney says with a laugh, hugging her tightly.

"Hey, isn't it true that witches celebrate Yule on the twenty-first of December?" Beth asks Kenosha. "Didn't we miss it?"

"Yuletide is twelve days, Beth," Kenosha says, shaking her head. "Many celebrate on the twenty-first, but many more celebrate at different times. In ancient times, pagans celebrated Yule for twelve nights. The Hawthorne coven under Alondra always celebrated throughout December, particularly on the last day. And, apparently, now under your new High Priestess—" She nods to me. "The Hawthorne coven celebrates Christmas Day too."

"We're all still getting together with the coven on the last night of Yule," Bryce says.

"It's an ice cream maker, Meer!" says Courtney. "Don't you just love it?"

"Thanks, Courtney," Mira says with a wry smile. "I guess."

No, she doesn't love it. It's really a gag gift, you know. You can't imagine how difficult it was to get those two here at my party to celebrate Christmas. Mira spends all year telling everyone how stupid and commercial Christmas is.

Melanie laughs at the gift. But then she just sits on the carpet with her back against the couch watching all our other friends open gifts. At times, I catch her glancing at me.

But then I realize she's not really looking at me, she's looking behind me. Behind my lounge chair the sliding glass door reveals the dark evening in my backyard. She probably would have preferred that we meet outdoors. Because she's a witch. No matter what she says, Melanie will always be a witch. And witches love the outdoors, even when it's cold.

I get up and walk over to her. Then I kneel.

"Melanie," I ask quietly, almost in a whisper. "Were you with me in the forest a few days ago? Or was that just a vision in my head?"

"When?"

"When I was fighting Grýla? I had a vision of you in our ice cream parlor. You helped me by suggesting we stop all our dark magic. You helped us."

Melanie shrugs.

"Well, if it was you, I really want to thank you. You saved Cat and all of Hawthorne."

Melanie shrugs again. Then Melanie laughs as Courtney opens Mira's gift. It's a jar of water with a label on it reading "Hawthorne Christmas snow."

"Thank you, Melanie, for saving us," I say. And I hug her.

"I thought it was your friends who saved you?" Melanie asks with a nod. "Walpurgis, Cadence. Walpurgis. And Merry Christmas."

14

HAPPY YULE

WHIFFS OF LOVELY APPLE AND CINNAMON MIST MOISTEN MY upper lip as I cup a small white mug in both hands by my face. As I walk, I'm drinking Abella's wonderful hot winter elixir. Umm, it's so yummy. It's a sweet apple cider. And the warmth on my face is so nice in the cold. But as we walk along the woodsy path, it's not just leaves and branches we're crunching with our flat black boots, you know, it's shards of ice. It snowed again last night.

Clouds pass by a half-moon overhead. A few snowflakes are still lightly falling among the trees, sprinkling more white fluff over our dirt forest path. I'm wearing two shirts, a sweater, and a witch robe with the hood over my head. So are all my other witches, because tonight in darkness, unlike so many other nights by our bonfire, our sabbath is done in walking meditation. But though walking, I'm still officiating with my coven.

"Blessed be," I say as we walk. "Blessed be the Hawthorne coven under Khione. *Lux alba et tenebris*. As we enter Yule, our longest night of darkness, look to your left and then look to your right." I turn to Bryce on my right and smile. Maddie, who's walking with Damie, cocks her head back and smiles under her hood in the white moonlight. "Although sight be dimmed, feel the warmth of each other through this blessed night. Our Yule season. Atman, witches."

"Atman," says Bryce, closing his eyes and nodding.

"Atman," echo the rest of my witches.

"And let Abbie's cider warm us through the fucking cold, Katesy," Maddie adds. "Brr, what a cold winter night."

We laugh.

"Sure, Maddie."

"Mira, just make sure you don't trip on the branches up there," Maddie hollers.

Mira and Courtney are leading this walking group. But they're not using flashlights, according to tradition.

"The moon is bright enough, Maddie," Mira says up ahead.

"Cadence needs to be careful with her baby," Bryce adds.

"I'm fine, Bryce," I say, rolling my eyes. But then my hubby reaches over to hold my free hand. And I love that.

"Witches," I say, returning to officiating, "darkness represents our longest evening. So when we walk, we don't only celebrate the blackness of night, we look forward to light. When in darkness in this season, we burn our Yule log. Fire from our logs represents the warmth that continues to burn into our new year. In ancient times, Yule logs were said to stay warm and bright for twelve days. Another tradition is the Yule Goat, where the city had to protect an effigy from arsonists. Why? Arsonists weren't just trying to destroy property. They wanted to burn the statue to bring the heat of the burning goat to the center of town to welcome the new year, guys. See, our warmth is like fire guarding us from the cold. Our togetherness. Let the love of this Hawthorne coven, our warmth together, cast away all our shadows."

"Atman, Windstorm," Mira says ahead of us, nodding.

"Atman," the High Wizard, my hubby, says with a nod.

"Katesy," Maddie says, "are you done doing your thing?"

"Sure, Maddie," I say with a laugh. "I guess."

"Well, you know Tammy is having her wedding in Jamaica? She and Nate are finally tying the knot. Ain't that fabs? That means that we all have to plan for the trip. She set a date between semesters so we could make it. Damie and I would love to invite as many of you as we can. I mean, we're all going, so I figure why not all of us go together and stay in the same hotel room, guys?"

"Maybe a couple hotel rooms," I object.

"Well, Katie can't go if she's too pregnant," Bryce says.

"I'll be fine, Bryce," I object, rolling my eyes. "Stop."

"We also have to still make it to New York City for Frida, guys," says quiet Helen, walking a couple witches behind me. "Don't forget she's getting married too."

"Don't get why y'all don't just go to city hall, sign papers, and be done with it," Mira says. "That's what Courtney and I did. Every time one of us gets married, it doesn't have to be all fancy-schmancy, like you and Katie's wedding."

"I thought their wedding was so beautiful, Meer," Courtney objects.

"Yeah, well."

We stop jibber-jabbering. And we walk in silence. But that's nice too. I let the steam rise from my cup along my cheeks and just walk. And it's soothing. With everyone silent, even all my quieter newbie witches, we all just crunch through leaves, branches, and ice along this broad dirt path, enjoying the sound of our boots.

"Just let Damie and me know," Maddie says. "It's easy-peasy planning for my responsible *doctor*."

Then she makes me nearly choke on my cider as she hugs and kisses my brother's lips in front of Bryce and me.

"Cat, this is what our coven is all about," I say, cocking my head back. She's following in the rear near Helen. "We just yap. Our weekly meetings are just about yapping."

"Sure, Cadence," Cat says. "No real magic ever happens in Hawthorne, right?"

We laugh.

"You guys are totally cool," Cat says. "And I totally want in the coven."

"After everything that happened?" asks Bryce.

"Yep. You bet I do."

"You can't, Cat," I reply. "I told you. There are too many witches in our coven already."

"Hey, I can see Josie's lights up ahead now!" interjects Beth. She's walking with Nancy, behind Cat. "We must be close!"

Bryce and I look. I have to squint without wearing glasses. I think Beth's right, I see a hazy yellow glow ahead.

"If you want into our coven so bad, ghost hunter, you can join," Mira says. "Helen, Josie, and Debra are graduating. We might need some of your friends next year."

"Shh!" I snap. "Come on, Mira. Don't get her excited." I put a finger over my lips, but I can't help but grow a smile due to Cat's enthusiasm. "Anyway, she needs to get into college first."

"I'm already in Hawthorne," Cat says. "I told you that, Cadence. But thanks, Raven, you know I'll do whatever I need to do to join. Do you guys do some weird initiation or something?"

In a large grassy glade, there are like a hundred small

yellow candles lit in a large circle. We're on a cliff, similar to campus's famous Hilltop Bluff, but smaller, and four witches from our coven, Josie, Abella, Noori, and Gail stand near a low, simmering bonfire surrounded by unlit torches. They are waiting for us with big smiles. On one side of me is the thick forest, but on the other is this cliffside on a high elevation over the woods. Shadows of Hawthorne woods spread out for miles below. I can't make out my house, but it's somewhere down there. But I do spot the university lights in the far distance. And, if I squint hard enough, I can just make out the small black shadow of Hawthorne Lake. On the very far reaches of the horizon, there are shadows of mountains. The fire and all these candles under us seem so bright on the darkest night, particularly after my eyes have adjusted to the darkness. And that, not only the maze, but *that* is the point, you know.

"*Yatu*, Windstorm," says Josie with a big grin. "So how'd we do?"

"*Yatu*, Andrena," I say, putting my arms around Josie. "Are you kidding? It's absolutely amazing!"

"Well, I had a lot of help from the others," Josie says with a laugh.

"Took us all day, Cadence," says Abella.

"It looks so great, guys. This cider is amazing too, Abie."

"Who walks in first?" Bryce asks me. "We have to go in one at a time. And remember to walk with one candle by your chest."

"I'd like to go," Mira says. "But . . . Courtney can go before me."

"Thanks, Meer." Courtney kisses her cheek.

"Remember, really focus," I say. "Ground yourselves. We probably shouldn't have been yapping so much coming over, but now it's too late. Anyone who enters needs absolute silence. Walk slowly and carry your flame. Add the candle to the central Yule log. Then, they say, by the center, if blessed by Hecate, you will have gnosis. But you must remain quiet. That means—" I turn to my best friend, Maddie, and she scowls. "No yapping outside the maze either, Maddie."

Maddie sticks her tongue out at me.

"Do we have your permission to enter, High Priestess? High Wizard?" Mira asks excitedly.

Bryce and I nod.

Then we all watch Courtney slowly grab a candle, and she walks in first. Mira walks in slowly after her.

In contemplation, they both slowly make their way through the circular maze of candlelight. I let all our witches add their fire to the center of the maze. Then, finally, I take one last sip of cider, put it on the ground, and light my small candle.

The first thing I love is the warmth of my single candle by my chest. Then comes my surprise at how long the labyrinth seems. Even though the hillside is not that large, the winding of the maze makes the labyrinth of light much larger than it appears from the outside. I focus . . . I concentrate. I ground myself in meditation, concentrating on my inner light, meditating, as my teacher once taught me to do. Soon, I wander with little thought. I know you're still beside me, but all else is quiet. My friends have heeded my instructions. No one is saying a word.

I discover the center of the maze and place my candle down. Then I gaze up at the bright half-moon.

"Blessed be," I say pensively, nodding my head and looking up into the clouds and the moon above. "Glory be to God."

"Happy Yule, Windstorm!" they all shout, hugging one another.

"Merry Christmas, guys."

THE END

WITCHY ADVENTURES ARE CONTINUED IN OTHER
BOOKS IN THE HAWTHORNE UNIVERSITY WITCH
SERIES

THE SERIES

- BROOMSTICK
- WINDSTORM
- THE HAWTHORNE WITCH
- WITCH MIRROR
- RAVENS
- SHADOW CAST
- BELTANE FIRE short story prequel
- SAMHAIN WITCH short story (3.5)
- CANDY CRONE (6.5)
- ALONDRA 20 yr prequel

THE BOXED SETS

- THE HAWTHORNE UNIVERSITY WITCH
  SERIES
- THE HAWTHORNE UNIVERSITY WITCH
  SERIES (4-6)
- THE HAWTHORNE UNIVERSITY WITCH
  HOLIDAY COLLECTION

AND DON'T FORGET THAT THE ENTIRE SERIES IS
NOW AVAILABLE ON AUDIO, PERFORMED BY ALEXA
ELMY AND PRESTON GEER!

ALSO BY A.L. HAWKE

PARANORMAL ROMANCE

- THE HAWTHORNE UNIVERSITY WITCH SERIES I-III
- THE HAWTHORNE UNIVERSITY WITCH SERIES 4-6
- THE HAWTHORNE UNIVERSITY WITCH HOLIDAY COLLECTION

- SHADES
- HAUNTING JOY
- PHANTOM MASQUERADE

- MY EVIL EYE
- THE GUARDIAN
- NECTAR OF AMBROSIA
- CORA

FANTASY: THE AZURE SERIES

- HARMONIA
- CORA: RISE OF THE FALLEN GODDESS
- AZURE BLUE
- CORAL RED
- PRINCESS SOJOURN

SCIENCE FICTION

- CANDY SAVANT SERIES

Books available at https://alhawke.com/books

PARTING WORDS

What did you think of *Candy Crone*? By placing a book review, you can inform others of your thoughts and help spread the word about my book.

Want more? Periodically I like to send news regarding current or new projects. If you'd like to be privy, I encourage you to sign up to my email newsletter. Your information will remain private and you can cancel any time.

Sign up at www.alhawke.com or scan the following QR code:

"CHAPTER 1 - HER AFFLICTION" IN
BROOMSTICK, BOOK 1 OF THE HAWTHORNE
UNIVERSITY WITCH SERIES BY A.L. HAWKE

I feel a chill in the air. But the sunlight flickers between fall leaves warming me as I walk across campus with my best friend, Madison. It will be winter soon, but for now, the last days of autumn in Georgia seem so peaceful. I glimpse at patches of blue through the canopy of trees. The sky is like ... so perfect. I love fall, I really do.

But Maddie doesn't seem interested in Mother Nature. She's been acting like a witch since we got up, which is a bit odd because my BFF is one of the most energetic and cheery girls I know. I already asked her what's wrong, but she won't tell me.

We pass the dorms and climb the grassy hill at the center of campus. At the summit is the tallest building at Hawthorne University: our library. But we're not checking out books. A line of students snakes its way through a bunch of cute tables with burgundy umbrellas to the counter of our university coffee shop. I think the wait takes Maddie over the edge.

She finally starts spitting out the events of her evening. "I went out on a date with Patrick. You know, the guy in my film studies class." She told me about him before, emphasizing how tall and cute he is, but now she looks as if she bit into something sour. "I knew there was trouble the minute he picked me up in that filthy, dilapidated flatbed truck." (I'm not surprised. She's not a very good judge of character, you know). "We had this great tilapia chili dish and lime-green margaritas and everything was going fine until he reached under my skirt and touched my vagina." I look around me, biting my lip nervously. We're still standing in line, and she said the word *vagina* really loud. People are turning to look. Then Maddie tells me she hit him on the head. Patrick, acting like he was the victim, jumped up from their booth, ran, and left her the bill.

Anyway, Maddie's busy telling me this story about her date copping a feel—and saying the word *vagina* real loud—when, right before my eyes, she walks into the store and just grabs a drink off the counter. We haven't ordered anything yet. It looks like a latte, but I'm not sure. I'm not so sure she knows either. Then she grabs my arm and we make a hasty exit. Maddie is like a total kleptomaniac.

As we walk down a cement path paralleling the grassy hill, I stare at her and she flashes a really sweet grin, raising her cup as if in a toast. "Anyway, fuck him."

I'm thinking, *At least she was asked out on a date.*

She looks at the brew in her stolen cup, puzzled. Then she throws her long hair back and cocks her head toward me very earnestly, saying, "Alondra wants to meet you."

I'm still looking at her in shock.

"Why not?" Maddie asks. "It'll be fun."

But I'm not thinking about Alondra. I point at her cup.

"It's really good," she says with a chuckle. "I think it has soy. Want some? I don't usually order soy but...this isn't bad. Look, Katie..." (People call me Katie a lot, even though my name is Cadence.) "Alondra says she wants to meet you outside of class. Just come with me to her house."

"I don't know," I say. "I don't like the look of her."

Now we're dodging bodies on the crowded lawn, heading to the main hall of the university. The main drag of Hawthorne is a white paved sidewalk surrounded by grass and trees, with brick buildings on both sides—and even more college bodies. The classroom buildings are spread out through the fields and under the tall trees. The leaves are so pretty in red and orange. Fall is my favorite time of year because I love the colors.

Hawthorne University is in Georgia. It's a really nice college, and I'm lucky to have been accepted here. So is Maddie. Everyone has a book tucked under their arm or is carrying a backpack. I have a pink backpack decorated with a unicorn. Maddie has always thought it's a little too cute, but I think it's whimsical. It even has purple swirls around the straps. Maddie's carrying a small book, but I'm pretty sure she won't read it. She's not the best student.

"You should go," Maddie says again, sipping her stolen drink. She runs her free hand through her hair, which is long and black like mine. I reach for my hair and realize I put it in a bun this morning, so I just pat the top of my head like an idiot. Then I think about Maddie's being a poor judge of character and think to myself, *No. No way am I going to Alondra's.*

"Why do you do that?" I point to her cup.

Then she drinks some more with a large grin. Again, she offers me some, but I don't have a chance to taste it because a nerdy-looking boy with glasses sprints between us, nearly knocking down her mysterious drink.

"Hey!" Maddie yells. "Watch where the fuck you're

going!" Then she turns back to me. "It's busy, Kate. We should have gone into town like I told you."

I shrug. "I thought we'd just spend the afternoon on the grass studying for midterms."

I must look hurt because Maddie giggles and runs her hand down my back. "Whatever. Whatever you want." Then she leans closer to me. "Just come with me tonight. Please. It'll be a lot of fun. Alondra's really nice. And I have a surprise."

"I don't know."

"Well…" Maddie walks off and stands under a really large tree. "You have to. For the surprise."

"Yeah? What?"

"Bryce will be there."

"So?"

"Whaddaya mean *so?*" she says. "You can't stop talking about him."

Of course Bryce will be there. He's my teaching assistant and is really hot. "You're just scared," I say. "Now you're trying to bribe me."

"I'm not scared, Cadence."

She plops down on the lawn, puts her book on her chest, and closes her eyes. I catch a glimpse of the book's cover. It features a burly man with rippling muscles and the title *Complete Me.* She's not studying.

"Just come," she says with her eyes closed. "I'll meet you back in our dorm at six to get ready."

"Are we eating there?"

"Yeah." Maddie laughs with her eyes still closed. "Alondra always has plenty to eat. Too much. She knows just how to fatten you up."

Dr. Alondra Johansen has a house in the middle of a thick forest, only a couple of miles from the university. It's rumored to have been built during the Civil War. I believe it. It's a white-columned two-story mansion with a large shaded patio and a beautiful paved walkway. It makes me think Scarlett O'Hara from *Gone with the Wind* is going to run down the steps, any minute, to greet us. Surrounding the walkway is a field of grass and tall trees, along with a garden full of white and red lilies. I like lilies. I don't like taking care of them, or any flowers for that matter, but I like looking at them. Especially in the wild. I like the outdoors. Always have.

A small wooden carriage, painted red, sits on a modern paved driveway alongside the property. Parked behind it is Dr. Johansen's dark gray Jaguar XJ. How does she own all this stuff? Some say she's the descendant of an old wealthy family. It can't be from her salary. She's my history professor.

There are others walking up the dirt walkway, mostly girls I recognize from class.

With all the grandeur of the mansion, I'm surprised to see Alondra herself greet us at the door. A long pitch-black cape is draped over a darker black silk shirt and slacks. She has long black hair like mine, hanging loosely in waves. This time I'm wearing my long hair down too. And like the times I've seen her in class, I'm struck by her eyes. Alondra has bright jade eyes, like jewels. Her skin is pale, much paler than mine, and for a moment I imagine that she's a vampire. It would certainly fit her affinity for the nineteenth century.

But her smile isn't sinister; it's sweet. She's always nice—too nice. She has a bright grin and seems thrilled to see me. "Cadence Hawthorne, come in." I'm a little surprised she remembers my name. "I'm so glad you came. Are you considering our project?"

"I'm thinking about it, Dr. Johansen."

Standing beside Alondra is her teaching assistant, the irresistibly yummy guy Maddie used to bribe me to come. Bryce's suit doesn't hide his muscular, athletic physique. He's looking down into my eyes too. But his eyes are blue— gorgeous blue. I'm reminded of the cover of that trashy romance novel my best friend was reading. The model was like a bulkier version of Bryce, but Bryce is the real deal— and incredibly hot.

Now I'm blushing.

"Cadence," Bryce says, taking my hand formally and tipping his head.

I'm cherry red.

Bryce turns to my friend. "Madison."

"Hi, Bryce," Maddie says. Then she looks at me and struggles not to laugh.

I look away.

The foyer is grand. Above me is this amazing chandelier. It's made of a hundred tiny crystals reflecting light. It's the most beautiful chandelier I've ever seen. I almost feel dizzy looking up at the twinkling crystals. But that doesn't do justice to the rest of the house. The hallway, including the wooden-railed stairway, is white, and marble columns frame the front door. Enormous windows extend from the ceilings to the travertine floor. The hallway leads to the kitchen, where everyone has gathered, their voices echoing through the house.

Dr. Johansen greets me as we linger just inside the door- way. "Please, call me Alondra." Oh yeah, my professor is still greeting me. Watching me. She's still looking at me with her mesmerizing green eyes. I completely forgot about her. I'm a little surprised she didn't say hello to Maddie. "You can reserve calling me by my title for when we're in class,

Cadence," she says with a nod. "But here, please relax. Call me Alondra."

Oh shit, do I not look relaxed?

My eyes fall on Maddie. My BFF bitch has the largest grimace I've seen in weeks.

"Come in, you two," Alondra says. "Make yourselves at home."

Make yourselves at home. And Alondra really seems to mean it. Bryce leads me to the kitchen, leaving the other two behind.

The kitchen is just as lovely as the entryway, with steel stoves, and marble—like *real* marble—countertops. It's all tidy and neat. About fifteen people are gathered in a small adjoining dining room, talking and laughing, their voices echoing through the large open spaces.

"You can help me with the trays," Bryce says with this amused smile. I catch his eyes straying along my shoulders and down my elegant black dress. It looks like he's thinking of something other than the trays.

What's on your mind, Bryce? … Hope it's me.

"Sure," I say.

He collects glasses already full of champagne and places them on two trays. "How do you like our class?" he asks.

"It's good. I especially like ancient history and medieval times."

"Yeah," he says. "You know, I used to be interested in engineering, but that changed when I saw how much math I'd need to know." He chuckles. I ogle his lips and that to-die-for strong jawline as he laughs. I freeze for a second. I fight off a blush and hope he doesn't notice. "I suppose that's what fascinates me about witch trials," he says.

"It's all…fascinating," I say. "You really seem to be into Dr. Johansen's research."

He lifts the tray and places it in my hands. I'm extra careful, because my heart is beating so fast staring at those thick biceps, and the last thing I want to do is drop the tray. But Bryce is so cute.

TO BE CONTINUED IN BOOK I OF THE HAWTHORNE UNIVERSITY WITCH SERIES

ABOUT THE AUTHOR

A.L. Hawke is the author of the bestselling Hawthorne University Witch series. The author lives in Southern California torching the midnight candle over lovers against a backdrop of machines, nymphs, magic, spice and mayhem. A.L. Hawke writes fantasy and romance spanning four thousand years, from pre-civilization to contemporary and beyond.

Visit A.L. Hawke at www.alhawke.com

Email: contact@alhawke.com

www.ingramcontent.com/pod-product-compliance
Lightning Source LLC
Chambersburg PA
CBHW021720190726
48289CB00008B/2622